LOVERS' KNOT

LOVERS' KNOT

Christina Green

CHIVERS
THORNDIKE

This Large Print book is published by BBC Audiobooks Ltd, Bath, England and by Thorndike Press®, Waterville, Maine, USA.

Published in 2005 in the U.K. by arrangement with the author

Published in 2005 in the U.S. by arrangement with Dorian Literary Agency

U.K. Hardcover ISBN 1–4056–3268–2 (Chivers Large Print)
U.S. Softcover   ISBN 0–7862–7428–X (Nightingale)

The text of this Large Print edition is unabridged.
Other aspects of the book may vary from the original edition.

Set in 16 pt. New Times Roman.

Printed in Great Britain on acid-free paper.

British Library Cataloguing in Publication Data available

Library of Congress Cataloging-in-Publication Data

Green, Christina.
    Lovers' knot / by Christina Green.
       p.   cm.
    ISBN 0–7862–7428–X (lg. print : sc : alk. paper)
    1. Devon (England)—Fiction. 2. Women travelers—Fiction.
    3. Large type books. I. Title.
    PR6057.R3378L68 2005
    823'.914—dc22   2004029246

CHAPTER ONE

She was home! Lisa Dorant paused in the street, outside the antique shop, and saw that the town had hardly changed at all since she went away eighteen months ago. Egypt, Greece, Spain and all the other holiday centres of the world had seemed so much more enticing then, and now she understood why. Stretton, in Devon, was small, insular and vastly different from the capitals where she had worked as a travel courier, but she was still glad to be back here, ready to greet her family with the fondness she'd always felt for them

Picking up her bag, a smile on her face, she opened and entered the shop expecting to see Martin, who must be running it now. Terry, her brother, was in hospital. But it was her sister-in-law, Sarah, who sat behind the counter, who looked up without an answering smile and said coolly, 'So you're here at last. Took your time, didn't you?'

Lisa felt her face flame. She dropped the bag, stared at Sarah and said crossly, 'That's not fair. When you phoned, telling me about Terry, I told you I had to make arrangements. I couldn't just walk out on my bosses. I came as soon as I could.' So, she thought angrily, don't I even get a welcome? But loud, she added, 'How's Terry? Can I see him this afternoon?'

Sarah put down the small price tag she was marking, glanced up and nodded. 'He's looking forward to your visit. I haven't been able to get to the hospital as often as I'd like— the shop, you see. And my job.' Her smile was tight. 'Like you, I couldn't just walk away from my class at school, could I? Holidays are here, but I've still got lots to do. That's why I phoned you. Why it's so necessary for you to be here, to help out.'

'But you've got Martin . . .' Lisa swung round. If she didn't break up this unwelcoming atmosphere she knew she'd say something she regretted. Sarah was without doubt a good wife to Terry and an excellent primary school teacher.

But she showed little warmth and Lisa knew that when Dad died, two years ago, Sarah and Terry had both expected her to help run the shop. There had been uncomfortable arguments about her leaving Stretton and following her ambition to become a travel courier.

She remembered her fervent words, even now . . . 'I can't stay here, Terry—I need different things than you do. I want to travel— that's why I've taken French and Spanish . . . can't you see?'

And Terry, bless him, had understood. 'Don't worry about it, Lisa love. Martin and I can cope, and Sarah will lend a hand in holiday

2

time.' So she'd left, not exactly happily, but knowing she must make a life for herself. And she'd kept in touch, sending postcards from strange and distant lands, telephoning from the continent, always aware that her family was still there in Stretton, established and safe, somewhere she could visit when she herself was on holiday.

And now this non-welcome from Sarah. Lisa turned again and looked at her sister-in-law's sharp features and big dark eyes and wondered for the umpteenth time what Terry had ever seen in such a laid-back and uncommunicative girl, given his own friendliness and understanding.

But if she'd learned one thing on her travels, it was that people all over the world are all different, indeed unique. Suddenly the idea of Sarah's reactions, told she was unique, seemed amusing, and Lisa found herself smiling into the cool dark gaze as she returned to the important reason for her home-coming. Concentrate on Terry, forget Sarah's unfriendliness.

'So tell me about Terry. How did it happen? Is he in pain?'

Sarah got up from her seat and went to the window, bending to run a carefully dusting hand around the pink Sevres plate that dominated the display of porcelain. 'He was cleaning the window and overbalanced. Simple as that. Fell and broke his leg. Both bones, a bad break, and he's in traction.' She straightened, glanced at Lisa. 'No, he's not in pain now. But having to be stretched out in that machine isn't exactly comfy. He can't even sit up.'

She hesitated, then added, her tone slightly higher, the words coming fast. 'I mean, I'd warned him about cleaning the windows so many times—Martin should have done it, but of course he was out, wasn't he? Wandering round the market like he always does on a Friday.'

Lisa said nothing, but regarded Sarah with new eyes. So there was some emotion after all, concealed beneath the elegant exterior and dismissive expression. And what was all this about Martin, who had always been such a treasure, right from the day Dad employed him on leaving school?

'It must have been a shock,' she said sympathetically, and Sarah turned, staring at her almost fiercely.

'Yes,' she said. 'A great shock. And that was when I really realised that you ought to have been here.'

'But we agreed.' Lisa was taken aback by the resentment in her sister-in-law's voice.

'Terry agreed, you mean, you know I didn't.' Sarah went back to her seat behind the counter and picked up another of the price labels. Lisa saw her hand shaking. 'I always felt that you were selfish and undisciplined to go

4

off, jaunting all over the world like that when you were needed here.'

'Jaunting?' Lisa almost gasped. 'It's my work, not a holiday! If you think being a travel courier is pure enjoyment then you're absolutely wrong. It's like coping with thousands of irritating school kids who expect you to know all the most unlikely answers and blame you if you don't.'

She saw the hint of a smile, before Sarah shrugged and continued to write prices on the small slips of card. 'You're family,' she said flatly. 'It was your duty to run the shop with Terry. Your dad left it to both of you, but you went off and left Terry alone.'

Now Lisa was getting angry. This was nonsense. She and Terry had talked it all over and when that first job was offered her, he'd said, 'OK, Lisa, I do understand. So off you go . . . and don't forget to send us a postcard from the jungle, or where ever you end up!'

Now she turned away from the counter and looked around the shop, relying on familiar sights and smells to cancel out the resentment she felt inside.

There had been slight alterations that she recognised at once. Redecoration, new shelves, a more up-to-date lighting system, and some unobtrusive closed-circuit cameras, but the atmosphere of remembered pleasure in beautiful artefacts remained the same.

The cabinet full of gleaming Victorian

5

jewellery still stood in the far corner and the portrait of the lady of the manor even more fleshly bare than she recalled.

For a second she almost expected Dad to appear, his old beige cardigan a bit baggier, his smile the warm and loving one that he dispensed throughout his small world.

Then the shop door opened and at once she swung around, smiling. 'Hi, Martin—' She was glad to see him if only to break up this wretched atmosphere between herself and Sarah. 'Good to see you again.'

He looked much the same as she remembered from their shared schooldays. Stockily-built with heavy shoulders, dark hair now cropped too cleanly to balance his rather sharp features.

But it was his eyes that caught her as they'd always done. Bright green and alert and full of something that, as ever, evaded her understanding. But at the moment they were welcoming and her own smile broadened in response.

He came to her side at once, pecked both cheeks and grinned. 'Hi, Lisa—yeah, great to see you . . . all tanned from foreign parts, eh?' She watched him look her up and down and felt relaxed at the sight of the appreciation on his face. 'Come to help out, right?'

Then his smile died and he glanced briefly at Sarah behind the counter. 'A bad show, poor old Terry cracking his leg. No one here when he did it, which didn't exactly help. Sarah at school, you see—'

Again he slid a glance towards her then returned quickly to Lisa. 'And I was doing errands, or something. Still, the ambulance came pretty quick and the medics soon got him to hospital. Going to visit, are you? He'll be pleased. Says it's dreary in there . . .' One dark eyebrow rose comically. 'Can't get his usual racing channel on TV, see? And all the others in the ward want to watch football!'

Lisa felt rejuvenated by this familiar chat. She and Martin had always got on well and now, after Sarah's less than welcoming words, his easy return to their old friendly relationship was stimulating. 'Sure, I'll see him this afternoon.'

She picked up her bag, walked past the counter, heading for the little room that led out of the shop, with just a glance in Sarah's direction. 'In the attic, am I? My old room? I'll go up and sort myself out . . . then you must tell me what I can do to help.'

Over her shoulder, she saw Martin's eyes following her, and at the same time noticed that Sarah was shrewdly watching him.

*   *   *

Her old bedroom—up in the attic of the 17th-century merchant's house in the centre of the little town—was much as she'd left it.

White-painted ceiling with ancient, tool-marked beams criss-crossing the ceiling and edging the walls.

She could see Sarah's elegant touch had been at work in the shape of bunches of colourful dried flowers hanging on the far beam and a handsome American patchwork quilt covering the single bed.

Lisa wondered wryly if the bumpy mattress she remembered from the past had been renewed too, and hoped so.

Once she'd unpacked, freshened up and changed into casual jeans and T-shirt, she went down to the kitchen and started preparing lunch. Sarah came in just as she was putting soup into pottery bowls. 'Martin's gone out—he'll be back later. Says he hasn't done the round of the market stalls yet—I've put up the closed sign.'

Her dark eyes were brooding, Lisa thought, and so, hoping to lighten the atmosphere, she said cheerily, 'Well, let me go into the shop when we've eaten. I'm sure you could do with some time to yourself. And then when Martin comes back I'll go and see Terry. I expect you'll be going this afternoon, won't you?'

To her surprise, Sarah shook her head. 'I've got the accountant coming round in a day or so, I must get the accounts sorted out. I'll see Terry this evening.'

As they ate in silence, Lisa tried again. 'Figures good, are they? Making a nice profit?

I remember Dad saying . . .'

Sarah cut in quickly, her tone sharp, eyes narrowing as she looked at Lisa. 'Your Dad didn't know his finger from his thumb, when Terry took over he found all sorts of discrepancies. We're still suffering from it today. Thank goodness I'm working. Things would be impossible if I weren't.'

'But surely Dad was good with figures? I remember how he helped me with homework.' Lisa didn't want to believe what Sarah had said. And once again, guilt caught her. Perhaps, after all, she should have stayed here, helped Terry sort out the financial mess—if indeed, a mess it was. Now she frowned, her voice tight as she said, 'What sort of discrepancies, Sarah? Bills? Bad debts? Exactly what do you mean?'

Sarah pushed her soup bowl away, ate the last crumb of her bread and cheese and rose. 'I can't go into it right now, Lisa. Like I said, I've got too much to do.' At the door she swung round, fixing her with a steely stare. 'And please don't talk to Terry about it. He's got enough to cope with as it is.'

'As if I would! I'm not stupid, you know!' Lisa plonked the empty plates and bowls on the draining board and tried to control her irritation. She managed to smile at Sarah before she left the room, and called after her, 'I'll be in the shop now, OK? I'll stay till Martin comes back.'

Sarah's voice drifted down the passage. 'Call me if you can't cope with things.'

CHAPTER TWO

In the shop Lisa sat on the same stool behind the counter that dad had always used and at once felt more relaxed. She reached behind her and there on the shelf was the same old book about antiques that she remembered from her childhood. Now she opened it and started reading while she waited for customers to arrive.

It fell open at a page of photographs of spectacular jewellery. Brooches, bracelets, hatpins, necklaces—Lisa felt a sudden stab of memory. That one looked very much like the wonderful old necklace that Dad had so much admired.

He'd always said it was his favourite—and it had a provenance, he insisted. Later than Victorian, and typically Edwardian, a relic of those spendthrift days when such gifts were commonplace among the aristocracy.

Lisa pictured it—a large, beautifully-crafted silver pendant on a matching chain, with tiny diamonds bordering the inset huge aquamarine that formed the pendant. And beneath the pale green aquamarine hung a small, elegant lovers' knot. It had been her favourite, as well.

She looked at the cabinet, in shadow by the far wall, and smiled. Yes, it was there, as gorgeous as ever, the centre of the display.

Leaning back, she could still hear Dad's voice. 'You may think it slightly vulgar, Lisa, love, certainly eye-catching, but to me it's incomparable. All that amazingly crafted silver, and then the huge aquamarine—takes a lot of beating.'

'Yes, of course, it would bring in a nice little sum, but my delight is in seeing it everyday, in the middle of the cabinet. And that's where it's going to stay.'

The doorbell jingled, bringing Lisa back to the present. She put away the book and looked up. A tall man came in, smiling as he met her gaze.

She took in the dark casual gear, thought he was good looking in a craggy sort of way and smiled back at him. 'Hi! Can I help you?'

'Hope so.' His voice was deep with a trace of a London accent. Lisa watched him pull a gold watch out of his jeans pocket. 'Is this worth anything?'

At once she recalled all Dad's advice. Don't do deals if you have any suspicions at all. Ask about provenance and look out for easy lies . . . Casually, she took the watch, handling it with care. 'It's a Hunter. Feels good.' The surface was smooth and shiny with age, and she turned it over in her hand. 'Let's open it— may I?'

The man nodded, watching her every move with intent pale blue eyes which seemed out of place given his casually tousled dark hair and strong eyebrows.

Something about his gaze made her feel uncomfortable, and she found herself hoping that he wasn't just trying on a quick scam. She concentrated on opening the back of the watch. Being with Dad in the shop on school holidays had taught her a few useful things. 'The movement's lovely,' she said, inspecting it carefully. 'Elegant. Yes, it's certainly worth something.'

Closing the watch she looked up and met his eyes. Now for the test. She lifted her chin. 'Family piece, is it?' This was the question Dad had told her always sorted the easy liars from the inarticulate truth tellers. What would this guy tell her? Wryly, she waited.

'No, just something I bought because I liked the look—and the feel—of it,' he said carelessly. 'Saw it when I thought I'd won the lottery—'

She couldn't resist the friendly, teasing smile. 'And did you? Win the lottery?'

'Would I be here right now if I had? No, I didn't.'

They grinned at each other. Then he asked again, 'Worth anything, is it?' and Lisa shot back to reality.

'Yes,' she said. 'Definitely. But I'm no expert. My colleague, Martin, can tell you more than I can, but he's out at the moment . . .' Martin had always specialised in jewellery and

13

she knew he'd love this watch.

The watch was being put back in his pocket. 'Martin?' asked its owner casually, and Lisa nodded. 'Martin Grainger. He helps my brother run the shop.'

The pale eyes looked her over appreciatively and she felt herself melt. This guy certainly was something—except that those eyes could get steely at times. 'And your brother is—?'

But right now they were super-friendly. No harm in telling him, thought Lisa, slightly dazed. 'Terence Dorant. He and I are owners.'

'So you're a Dorant too?'

'Lisa Dorant, yes.'

'And I'm Tom Fallon. Hi!' A large and powerful hand took hers and pressed it warmly. Lisa's smile grew. If this was the way life in dull old Stretton was going, she was glad to be here.

'I'll come back. See you soon—' A wave, a last grin, and Tom Fallon was gone.

Ridiculously, she felt a sense of absence and at once busied herself in turning the pages of the book in front of her.

*　　　*　　　*

Terry lay in his bed in the small, four-bedded ward, his right leg stretched out before him, enclosed in a series of bars and rods and weights. He smiled fondly at her. 'So good to see you Lisa, love,' he said. 'When Sarah told me she'd contacted you I didn't like the idea of hauling you back from where ever in the world you were, but now you're here—well, it's just great.'

He tried to move and she watched how uncomfortable the effort was. 'Sorry I can't get up and hug you,' he said wryly, 'but you see the position . . .'

Lisa bent down and kissed his cheek wishing she had a magic wand. Of all people, Terry was the last to accept immobility. A sportsman at school he still played golf when he could get away from the shop. 'Oh love,' she said softly, 'I'm so sorry.'

He nodded and grinned. 'So am I. Still, there it is. Teach me not to do things better left to younger, more flexible bodies. Never mind. Now—tell me about you.'

'I'm fine.' Lisa laughed. 'Glad to come back into nice warm, wet Devon for a change—jungles and deserts can be quite uncomfortable, you know!'

He grinned again, but she saw new lines of frustration on his face. Of course he must be anxious about the business . . . 'Terry,' she said firmly, 'you mustn't worry about things. Martin and I are coping in the shop now. Honestly, it's all going well.'

He looked at her for a moment without answering and she wondered suddenly at the look in his wide set hazel eyes. 'Yes, well,

Martin's very knowledgeable, thank goodness,' he said at last.

Lisa stayed for a while, chatting about the past, telling him some of the more amusing episodes of her work with tourists, and finally left knowing he looked more relaxed and less of a fish out of water than when she'd arrived.

*   *   *

Leaving the hospital, she crossed the road and started walking down the hill. Looking at her watch she saw that it was past closing time. Great, she thought—no need to rush back— I'll take a turn along the river path. It'll be like old times.

The June sunshine gleamed on the slow-flowing, grey-green water and the boats moored along the riverbank lifted and sank with the gentle rhythm of the current. Lisa felt her steps slowing too, her body and mind relaxing as the pace of life eased, joining in with that of the natural world.

She saw a couple coming towards her, a tall man and a girl reaching up to his shoulder, looking intensely at each other, talking as they walked. The man lifted an arm, his large fist striking the air, making a point. And the girl smiled up at him, clearly agreeing.

They looked like lovers in complete accord, thought Lisa. As they neared, she prepared a friendly smile, but then suddenly paused in her

16

stride. The man was Tom Fallon, and he was looking down at the girl beside him with what seemed to be great concentration. So great, in fact, that he passed Lisa without even looking her way.

She heard a few words, quick and clear, his voice deep and intent, before they moved out of earshot. 'We'll do it together, Debbie. Don't worry—I'll be right there with you.'

Lisa walked on, no longer enjoying the surroundings. Her thoughts raced. So Tom Fallon had a girlfriend. That was quite obvious and it was absolutely nothing to do with her. She felt her smile die, knew a sense of ridiculous disappointment and near resentment, before shrugging it away. This Tom Fallon meant nothing to her. So forget him. Easy!

It wasn't quite so easy. The fact of having seen the intimacy between Tom and his girl opened a shutter in her mind which had been carefully closed for the last few years.

She'd had boyfriends, of course, several and with varying degrees of affection. But there had been no-one really special.

Until today, when Martin had kissed her and welcomed her home, and she'd felt she was sliding back into their younger relationship—friends with perhaps a hint of something deeper to come.

She was fond of Martin, always had been and she was grateful for his welcome. But was he the one for her? Suddenly she realised that

17

her life, for all its busyness and excitement, had been lacking one thing—a permanent, satisfying relationship. Is this what she was hoping to find with Martin?

She turned off the path, walked rapidly back through the town and into the back entrance of the shop, thankful that he wasn't there, hoping Sarah was busy, for she needed time to think.

*   *   *

Going downstairs to see what was happening about supper, Lisa determined to stop being maudlin and make the best of whatever life brought her.

Right this moment it was a chicken sandwich, a mug of coffee and something bright on the telly. That should last her until Sarah came home and they could make plans for the future.

But, even as she sat down, the phone rang. It was Pearl Adams who ran the Costume Emporium just up the street.

'Lisa darling! I've just heard on the grapevine that you're home—come round for supper: why not? It's ages since I've seen you . . . I've got a casserole in the oven so we can sit and chat over a glass of wine until it's cooked. I bet you've got masses to tell me! See you in a minute, then?' The familiar voice with its wheezy laughter brought a smile to Lisa's

18

face.

Gratefully, she said, 'Pearl, that'd be fantastic. I'll be right round. Cheers.' At once the world was a degree brighter. Pearl had always been a cheering influence ever since Mum died and her friend, Pearl, had taken over the role of surrogate mother.

Lisa went downstairs to leave a message for Sarah who must be visiting Terry.

'Supper with Pearl. Don't wait up, love Lisa,' she wrote, and wished the 'love' didn't sound so forced.

CHAPTER THREE

Like the antique shop, Pearl's narrow, tall house had probably been the home of a rich merchant in the seventeenth century. Lisa found the back door ajar, with a luscious smell welcoming her into the kitchen where Pearl, fuzzy hair dyed the familiar raven-black and resplendent in a sweeping floral Laura Ashley skirt topped with a demure grey Edwardian blouse, pleated and buttoned to the neck, gathered her into one of the warm reassuring embraces Lisa had valued so much since her mother died.

'Come and sit down, darling!' Pearl busied herself at the Aga for a moment, checking on the casserole, tasting, adding herbs, and finally saying, as she sank into a creaky cane chair opposite Lisa, 'Another half hour and it'll be ready.

'Now my love, get this down you—' She poured red wine into two large glasses and pushed one along the table to Lisa. '—and tell me all about your adventures.' Her bracelets clinked, brown eyes sparkled, and at once Lisa lifted her glass. 'Here's to you, Pearl—it's so lovely to see you again.'

'And you, darling.' Pearl's astute gaze flickered up and down. 'Hmm, you've lost weight, but then you were always an eyeful, and now you've got that trendy short cut you look even more glamorous!' Her loud laugh filled the room. 'And from all I hear young Martin is delighted to see you back.'

Lisa's smile faded. 'Why d'you say that Pearl?'

'My dear, he's been counting the days since you left! Or so he's told everybody! Surely you know that?' Pearl's voice quietened and her eyes were shrewd. 'But obviously you don't— so why's the silly boy been bragging that you've got some kind of understanding between you?'

Lisa put down her glass. She couldn't believe any of this. For a moment she was silent. Then she said, 'Martin and I have always been friends, but never anything more,' she said, picking her words carefully. 'And no, there isn't any sort of understanding.'

Pearl shrugged and ran ringed fingers through her hair. Her smile flashed out again. 'Silly me! Must've got it wrong then—just gossip, I suppose, and nothing in it. Never mind! So tell me what Egypt was like—did you ride a camel?'

By the time Lisa had recounted various exciting and amusing bits of her working life, the meal was ready. And still they talked. Local gossip, memories of happy days in the past, ideas and hopes for the future.

Then, after one of Pearl's rich and sensuous puddings, followed by coffee and brandy, Lisa looked at her watch with a shock.

'Eleven! Can't believe it! The time's flown.' She got to her feet. 'Thanks, Pearl, for a super meal.'

At the door they embraced and Pearl said tentatively, almost as if she didn't want to say the words—'Lisa darling, if you find Sarah a bit difficult, do try and be patient. She's got a lot on her shoulders these days.'

'I know,' Lisa told her quietly. 'Such a worry, with Terry ill and the responsibility of running the shop, as well as her school work.'

'Not just that.' Pearl's usually loud voice was restrained and Lisa's eyes widened as she registered the suddenly serious expression. 'I mean financial worries, too.' Silver bracelets tinkled again, as Pearl shrugged, and then added, 'I fear we all exchange bits of news on the grapevine as you know, darling.' For a moment she paused. 'And the truth is I've heard that your shop isn't doing at all well.'

Lisa shook her head disbelievingly. Then she recalled what Sarah had said about low profits and discrepancies in the accounts after Dad's death. But Pearl was watching, and so she kept her expression impersonal.

Pearl was a real friend, but gossip could so easily get out of hand. So she gave her a last hug, saying brightly, 'Well, that's how it goes, I suppose. Up one year, down the next. I must run now, Pearl. Thanks again, and I'll see you soon. Cheers.'

Had Martin really said they had an

understanding? Rubbish, of course! Halfway home, she said aloud, in an angry voice, 'What a nerve!' and then was startled.

A figure approaching her stopped at her side and asked, 'Sorry—what did you say?'

She stared through the evening shadows and saw pale eyes, heard the familiar voice, and caught her breath. 'Oh! It's you!'

Tom Fallon frowned, bent a bit nearer. 'Sure it's me—but who're you?'

'Lisa. From the antique shop.' She was flustered now, keen to get away. What must he think of her, talking to herself?

But he put a hand on her arm, gently drawing her towards a lighted window a few steps away. 'Yeah, so it is—hi, Lisa!'

He smiled and she thought what an interesting, lived-in face he had. 'You're out late. No one to bring you home?'

'No. That is—no—'

'So may I walk you back? Just along here, isn't it?' Already he'd turned, waiting for her to agree.

Lisa was intrigued. She was quite enjoying this surprise meeting—particularly as Tom Fallon's girlfriend wasn't with him. So she walked along the street at his side and smiled as she asked, 'What happened to your lovely watch? Did you see Martin about it?'

Tom Fallon said casually, 'I saw him, yes, and I'll see him again tomorrow—he's consulting a mate about its value.' He turned his head to look at her, and she imagined the pale eyes seemed suddenly ice-cold. For a second a shadow fell over her. But then he added, 'Shall I see you, too, in the shop?' and his smile relaxed her again.

'I'll be there,' she said, halting at the gate leading to the small yard behind the shop.

'Cheers, then, Lisa,' Tom said.

'Cheers,' she echoed, and heard him walk away. Only when she realised he'd quite gone did she go into the house, lock the door, and creep quietly upstairs to her bedroom.

*　　*　　*

On Monday, she and Martin were in the shop together. Sarah said she would be home for lunch and they could both have a couple of hours off afterwards.

Then she wanted to go and visit Terry, so they must be back in the shop until closing time. Lisa thought this was a sensible arrangement. After all, she'd come home to help run the business.

It was a busy morning and it didn't take her long to get back into the swing of things. Nothing very much had changed in the way customers came in, selected, bought and paid for items.

But it soon became very clear that Martin had changed. No longer was he the overgrown schoolboy she remembered, of course, she hadn't expected him to be—but this new maturity, this keen observation of everybody and everything, added to a very obvious ambition, made him someone new to work with.

He slid an arm around her shoulders. 'Lisa, I'll teach you how to work the till? It's a state-of-the-art thing—look, like this . . .'

She didn't like the teach bit, and wanted to joke about the creaky drawer that used to double as a cashbox, but saw, from the gleam in his eyes, that it wouldn't amuse him any more.

And she noticed that he was treating customers differently from the way Dad had requested. Yes, a smile, but not a welcoming one. More a lift of the lips while the eyes remained cool and impersonal.

She decided to question him about the gossip Pearl had mentioned. 'Martin, here's your coffee. Time for a break, isn't it?' She put the mugs on the counter and sat on Dad's stool, grinning at him as he carefully rearranged some Georgian glasses on a shelf at the side of the shop. 'I saw Pearl last night,' she said casually. 'Heard all the latest chat—you know what she's like.'

Martin turned, took his coffee mug and stood between counter and door and she thought for all his average height, he had enormous attraction. He grinned at her. 'I certainly do! She's got it all worked out.

25

What's the buzz, then?'

Lisa sipped her coffee and eyed him over the rim. 'You and me, believe it or not!'

'What's that supposed to mean?'

She expected his easy grin to die but it didn't and she felt he wasn't taking it seriously enough. 'Just what it says—gossip about you and me? Now, who started that, I wonder?' she said tartly. 'Couldn't have been me, I wasn't here ...'

Inside her something uncomfortable nudged. She knew the old Martin would have instantly shaken off local gossip but suddenly he looked as if her words held no surprise.

He grinned broadly. 'Old Mother Pearl, eh?' Putting his mug on the counter, he leaned across it and ran a finger down her cheek. 'OK, so I've always had a thing about you, Lisa—maybe I told someone who told Pearl Adams ...' He shrugged.

Lisa edged out of his reach and said, a little stiffly, 'So why not tell me, too?'

Martin looked at her very hard. 'Sorry,' he said. His grin was quick, full of charm, and her irritation vanished as he went on, 'I mean, you've been back home for what, five minutes? And we've only had time to say hi, haven't we?'

He leaned closer across the counter, reached for her hand and stroked the palm with his thumb. 'Give me a chance, Lisa,' he said and his voice deepened. 'We've both

26

grown up a bit, haven't we? I guess we've got new things to learn about each other.'

A pleasurable warmth relaxed Lisa. She slid her hand away from his, but smiled as she said, 'You're right. And yes, like you say, we have to find out how we both feel now.'

His expression was bright. She thought he looked relieved and was touched by the idea that he really had been waiting for her to come back.

Then the doorbell chimed and he stepped away from her. The young woman entering walked to the counter and smiled at her and instantly Lisa recognised her as Tom Fallon's girlfriend, Debbie.

But this morning the anonymous anorak gear was replaced by an elegant trouser suit in a subtle, tawny shade that emphasised highlights in the bright chestnut hair, giving an expensive persona to the girl she had seen so briefly by the river yesterday. Forcing her thoughts aside, Lisa asked, 'Can I help you?'

'I've got a strange request to make,' said the girl with a friendly smile. 'Do you ever hire out jewellery?'

Quickly Lisa glanced across at Martin, who nodded briefly as he walked to the girl's side. 'Not normally,' he said briskly, his own smile responding to hers. 'But perhaps on occasions—it depends.'

'Well, this really is an occasion—let me explain.'

Lisa watched the girl turn towards him, clearly intending to charm him into acquiescence. Debbie was Martin's height and she was looking directly into his curious eyes.

Her voice was soft and a bit husky. 'It's for a publicity drive, you see—to advertise the Elizabethan fair at the end of the month, which of course is for charity. The sponsors would pay well and you'd get lots of PR for the shop.' Lowering her voice, 'Perhaps we could talk about it?'

Intrigued, Lisa saw that Martin needed no more persuasion. He stepped closer, taking control of the situation. 'Of course. This way—' He gestured to the room behind Lisa. 'We'll be private in here.'

Opening the door into the inner room, he let the girl precede him. Then she met Martin's eyes as he nodded at her before closing the door behind them. And she knew what his keen expression meant—'Don't interrupt us.'

A feeling of resentment grew in Lisa's mind. Martin was behaving as if he owned the shop. Of course, she understood that he'd obviously had to become a sort of managing figure since Terry's accident, but even so . . . now she was home, surely Martin must understand that she was a partner, while he was still only a member of staff?

Then she grew cross with herself, she and Sarah—and Terry—were lucky to have someone like Martin who could handle the business so competently.

*　　　*　　　*

Lisa lost track of the time of the private interview then, for trade became brisk and It was with a start of surprise that she heard the inner door open, and had to stand aside to let the girl and Martin come back into the shop.

Martin was smiling, standing a pace too close to Debbie, who smiled back and looked like the cat who'd just had the cream. Lisa pursed her lips. She wanted very badly to know what was going on, but obviously neither of them was about to tell her. Again, resentment flared, and she said loudly, to no-one in particular, 'Time to shut up for lunch, I think.'

Martin looked over his shoulder and gave her a terse stare. That made her blood start to simmer, so she added, even more loudly, 'You'll lock the door, won't you, Martin?' as she retreated into the inner room, making sure that she gave the smiling girl a hard look before shutting the door behind her.

She stirred up the pot of soup waiting on the back of the Aga, grabbed some bread and thought that Martin would have a lot of explaining to do, both to her and to Sarah if he was really allowing expensive pieces of jewellery to go out on hire just for the sake of some PR—and because of that wretched girl's smile. And as for Tom Fallon's girlfriend, well, she definitely didn't think much of her, smart gear or not.

And then the unwelcome thought insisted that Tom Fallon was nothing to do with her. Her frustration grew. Scowling, she wished she was back in Egypt. Or in the desert. Even in John O'Groats . . .

Martin didn't appear during the lunch hour and Lisa grew increasingly annoyed at his absence. Surely he could have come and told her what arrangements he'd made with that girl? Well, he'd certainly have to tell Sarah later this afternoon.

She cleared up her lonely meal without knowing she had done so, and then went up to her bedroom to brush her hair and think about the free couple of hours awaiting her.

Suddenly she felt alone and out of things . . . if Martin was really truthful about wanting them to spend time together he was going a funny way about it. Well, if he'd missed out on lunch it was nothing to do with her. She left the shop by the back door and marched down the High Street.

The sound of a guitar being expertly played made her look across the road. A busker leaned against the house opposite, drawing gentle, insistent tunes from his guitar. His face was turned down to watch busy fingers, but at once Lisa recognised Tom Fallon.

She drew in a startled breath and stood,

staring. An out-of-work musician? He sounded very professional—so why play here, with his cap on the ground, inviting donations? And if that elegant girl in the trendy suit was still his girlfriend, then what did she have in common with a shabby busker on the street?

Unable to answer any of these irritating questions, Lisa strode across the road, found a ten pence in her pocket and dropped it into Tom Fallon's cap. 'Lovely music,' she said, and watched him smile as he recognised her. The tune ended and the guitar was carefully put aside.

'Lovely audience,' he said quietly. 'Good to see you again, Lisa.'

For a moment she was off-balance. Those silver-blue eyes were warm and welcoming—or was she imagining it? And why should she feel like this when she'd just told Martin she was ready to pick up the old threads?

'I was—just—walking—er, doing some shopping . . .' The ridiculous excuses came out wobbly and hesitant.

But he nodded and bent to pick up his cap, counting the coins before pocketing them, and then giving her an amused grin. 'I'll never be rich. But money's not everything, is it?' And then, before she could answer, he swung the guitar strap over his shoulder and put a hand on her arm. 'How about a coffee?'

'Yes. I'm not due back in the shop till four . . .' why was she telling him this?

'Great. Let's go.' He took her arm crossing the street, opened Meg's Cafe door and followed as she entered.

Lisa saw familiar couples filling the tables and instantly thought of the local gossipmongers. 'Shall we go in the garden?' she suggested. 'It's got walls, so it's very sheltered.'

'Why not?' The blue eyes twinkled. 'I guess those walls are full of secrets . . . let's add to them, shall we?'

She laughed, but didn't know why. Secrets? Just a funny thing to say, of course. Why should she and Tom Fallon have secrets? And then nothing mattered, because they sat in a sunny corner with purple clematis climbing the warm brick wall behind them, and Meg was putting plates of luscious cakes and mugs of coffee on the small table, and Tom was still smiling at her . . . and, yes, she felt even more relaxed—even happy.

Happy—the first time she'd felt like this since she'd come home. But it was wrong, because she should be with Martin—feeling happy with Martin, not with this stranger, Tom Fallon.

Her smile fell away, and of course he noticed. She knew instinctively that Tom was the sort of man who noticed everything.

'Something wrong, Lisa?'

She pulled herself together. 'No, this is great—I was at a bit of a loose end.' He was looking at her with what she felt was warm understanding. She needed to explain, to express some of the strange feelings. 'It's funny, coming home after so long—and trying to fit in again . . .'

'I'm so sorry about your brother. But he'll be OK before too long, won't he? A bad break, wasn't it?'

How did he know? Then she thought again of the local gossip network. 'Yes, but he's getting on all right.' A pause and she caught hold of her courage. 'Where do you live? Locally?'

Another pause, but only for a second. 'Down by the river. I've got a flat. Here—' He pushed the plate of cake across the table. 'Have another bit. Good, isn't it?'

Was he changing the subject? She tried again. 'And do you busk here regularly? Other places, too?'

He looked down at his mug, stirring sugar into it. 'That's right. Plymouth, Exeter, all good venues for down-and-outs like me. Trouble is, guitar players are two a penny . . . I don't make much of a living.'

'But you play so well. Do you do professional gigs as well?'

He didn't answer at once and she had a weird idea that she was asking too many questions. Hurriedly, she said, 'Sorry, tell me to mind my own business . . .'

'Mind your own business, Lisa Dorant . . .'

33

But the smile was vivid and went right through her. 'OK, enough abut me—your turn now.'

She told him about her job as a travel courier, of her adventures all over the globe, of how good it was to be home again—but just a bit weird, too. Terry in hospital. The shop.

Tom was a good listener, asking questions, nodding as she explained, and then inviting her to have some more coffee. She waited for what might come next, but if she expected more personal information, she was disappointed.

'Your colleague, Martin Grainger,' he said slowly. 'Be back in the shop by now, will he? I said I'd call in and see if he's come up with a value for the old Hunter.'

Lisa nodded. 'We're both taking over from Sarah—that's Terry's wife—at four o'clock. She's going to the hospital.'

Tom glanced at his wrist. 'Better get a move on, then. Nearly four already. Finished, have you? Let's move . . .' He paid the bill, shaking his head when she offered to pay her way, and followed her out on to the pavement.

Together they walked up the High Street, passing Pearl's shop on the way. Lisa was immediately aware of eyes watching and voices chattering and felt angry about this local interest. Again, she wished she were back in her job—discovering new places, and new clients.

Tom stopped outside the shop, opened the

door and followed her in. Martin stood behind the counter and Lisa met his curious gaze with a very straight stare.

No need for him to look like that, as if she were his property and had no right to be out with anyone else.

She passed him on her way towards the small back room. 'I'll just go and get rid of my shopping . . .' There wasn't any shopping, but for some reason she didn't want to watch Tom Fallon and Martin talking together.

In the kitchen she looked at her reflection in the mirror and saw fierce grey eyes and patches of colour on her cheeks. Quite becoming, but not characteristic. Where had the gentler, more tolerant Lisa gone all of a sudden? It was a question she had no wish to answer—not at the moment, but as she calmed down, she foresaw a time, quite soon, when things might well come to a head between herself and Martin. In fact, probably this very evening.

CHAPTER FOUR

'Look,' Martin said, coming in from the kitchen, spooning second helpings of pasta onto her plate and pushing across the tomato sauce. 'No need to get so upset about if. She's only a customer, for heaven's sake.'

Lisa reached for the grated Parmesan and sprinkled it over her pasta. 'So why all that secrecy stuff? I'm part of the business too, you know. Salt, please—'

'Because she obviously expected some sort of personal treatment. After all, it's not every day that someone comes in suggesting they'll pay a whacking deposit for just hiring a bit of antique jewellery, is it?'

Sitting down, he filled their glasses with red wine and raised his towards her. 'Come on, Lisa love—don't be so touchy! This is supposed to be our get together, right? Drink up—here's to us.'

She smiled because she couldn't resist the invitation. It was cosy here in Martin's flat, he was a surprisingly good cook and the wine was really special. 'Sorry. I'll try and do better from now on. So tell me what Sarah said when you told her—'

Martin's dark eyebrow shot up wryly. 'Shouts and glares at first,' he said, grinning. 'Until I made her realise how much good it'll do the business to play the biggest part in the fair. Our name will be all over the town if the Queen wears our jewellery. Then she calmed down a bit. More pasta?'

'No thanks.' Lisa sat back. 'That was good.' She picked up her glass, looking at him over the rim. 'Which bit of jewellery was it? You didn't say—'

'The one your dad made such a fuss about. The aquamarine thing, remember it?' His voice was very casual, but he didn't meet her eyes.

Lisa put down her glass. She frowned. 'The Lovers' Knot piece? You must be joking! We can't possibly let that out on hire—I mean, Dad always said it was worth quite a bit. What on earth were you thinking of?' Anger and uneasiness prickled her. She didn't like the idea of Martin making such a big decision without telling her.

A silence grew and lengthened until he looked up and said, with a flash of annoyance, 'I was thinking of the good it'd do the business, to see that piece in public—it'll bring new interest to the shop . . . Why're you being so awkward? I bet your dad would've jumped at the chance . . .'

'He certainly wouldn't! He thought a lot of that necklace.' Lisa countered. 'And if it was worth a bit when he was alive, well, the price must've gone up by now. What about the insurance we'll have to pay? If all Sarah tells me is true, we can't afford it.'

'Sarah? Told you what?' Suddenly he sounded belligerent and Lisa's mind switched from lovers' knots to bills and discrepancies. She decided that Martin didn't need to know about the financial position and so she changed the subject very quickly.

'You said something about the fair, d'you mean the Elizabethan fair that happens every year? The one celebrating the old Queen's visit to Stretton in fifteen hundred and something? We always went to it, didn't we?' She grinned at him. 'I remember you dressing up as a peddlar and riding a Dartmoor pony— and nearly falling off!'

She saw Martin remembering, too. Pushing away his plate, he returned her mischievous grin. 'We go back a bit, don't we, Lisa? Well, maybe we can pick up the strands again this year. If Debbie's going to be the Queen of the fair this year, all glammed up and advertising our jewellery, I reckon we can get into the picture, too. How about being her lady-in-waiting? And I rather fancy playing the prince who wants to marry her!'

Their laughter flowed. Martin got up, put a disc on the music centre and then held out his hand. 'Come over here. This sofa's ancient, but comfy.'

Lisa sank down into the cushions and looked around her. The music was sweet and slow and relaxed her.

Martin's home was interesting and showed how he'd changed since their school days; clearly, he'd sloughed off the casual image she recalled, and was becoming someone who cared about antiques.

He'd obviously inherited one or two of his late mother's pieces of old furniture; but then she recognised the bureau against the far wall as eighteenth century Sheraton and the sofa she sat on was actually a rather nice Victorian chaise-longue, upholstered in silk weave, with pale striped cushions. But over there was a 1970's painted chair! It struck her it was a bit strange to see such a mixture of old and new.

She turned to look at him as he came and sat beside her. 'This is brilliant. Congratulations, Martin. I had no idea you'd grown so traditional in your tastes!'

His hand reached for her. 'Any chance of being traditional together?'

She smiled. Apart from the business of the jewellery, the evening was working out well so far, but the fact that he'd decided to hire out the Lovers' Knot pendant without consulting either her or Sarah still rankled.

Perhaps this was the moment to remind him that she and Terry were the owners, while he was just an employee. But that was an unkind way of putting it.

She sought for less aggressive words. 'Martin, look—I have to say this . . .'

He pulled his hand away and she saw the

easiness on his face fade. 'Sounds bad news. What've I done? Back to that jewellery thing, are we?'

'Don't be silly.' She laughed, but it didn't ring true. 'Actually, yes—and also—just that—well, please remember that the shop belongs to Terry and me.' As soon as she'd said it she thought how rotten she was being. He must think her a jumped-up snob and a particularly cruel one, remembering their old friendship.

'While I'm just the dogsbody—' Momentarily his voice was sharp, but then he smiled ruefully, grinning as he'd done in the old days when they'd had a quick flare-up of conflicting personalities, and then made up just as swiftly.

'I didn't mean it like that.' She took a reassuring sip of wine. 'But it's the truth, isn't it?'

Martin pursed his lips, swirled his wine around the glass and watched the liquid move. 'At the moment, yes, Lisa.' He glanced at her and she saw, with a start, how his eyes were suddenly keen and cool. 'But it won't be for ever. You see, I've got plans, and they include you. Look—'

Lisa caught her breath. She didn't like any of this. What was he talking about? Sounded as if he planned to take over the business—and her! He seemed so sure that she'd fall in with whatever he suggested—so what about her independence?

40

Tartly, she said, 'Hey, just remember I make my own plans, Martin. And don't imagine I haven't got any . . .'

They stared at each other and again she was back in the past, telling him what a nerd he was, and in a moment he would shout at her and then they'd sulk for five minutes before turning and grinning and making up. But that was then. This was now—and suddenly things felt very different.

Martin put down his glass, moved nearer and, reaching across, turned her face towards him. 'You're very beautiful when you're angry,' he murmured and his smile reminded her of how fond she'd always been of him.

When he drew her closer, she went willingly, closing her eyes and waiting for the feel of his lips on hers.

'Don't let's quarrel, Lisa. We've got too much going for us, haven't we?' His voice, whispering in her ear, was persuasive.

Dreamily, she nodded. This was what she needed, companionship, a man whose plans included her—so why did the doubts remain? 'Martin,' she said, a bit breathlessly as she pulled away, 'I'm not sure . . .'

'You soon will be.' There was abrupt confidence in the words, and as he released her, she saw an expression of raw ambition fill his face, turning him into someone she didn't want to know.

Instinctively she sprang to her feet. 'Sorry, I

think I must go—'

He stared, unbelieving. 'Why? What's wrong?'

She must get out. Why? No idea. Just—go. 'Sorry, Martin,' she muttered, heading for the stairs.

He saw her to the door, saying coldly, 'See you, then. Cheers,' and she walked away confused, embarrassed, but strangely certain that she'd done the right thing.

And yet—why this sudden need to escape? Maybe it was simply that they'd grown apart and it would take more than one evening together to adjust their developing personalities.

Without knowing it, she walked up the hill to the castle ruins, where she and Martin had always met in the past. Sitting down and watching the last shafts of sun fading, leaving the old stones dark and slightly sinister in the twilight, she thought about Martin's kiss.

What was wrong with her? She sank into a reverie, wishing she hadn't come home after all. If only tomorrow she could pack her bag and leave—the idea brought a smile back to her face.

Time to go home, but only Sarah would be there, full of fury about Martin's bossiness. Lisa stood for a doubtful moment before rapidly deciding on her next step. She'd call in on Pearl. Her kitchen would be warm, there would be coffee and gossip to help her forget these stupid worries.

'Darling—come in! What a lovely surprise. Mind you, I'm desperately busy.' Pearl drew her into the kitchen, reaching for the bottle of wine on the table. 'You can give me a hand, if you like. It's the fair, you see—now the posters are out and the local paper's going on about it, seems the whole of Stretton wants to find some ancient clothes and dress up!'

Lisa shook her head as the wine bottle turned in her direction. 'No thanks. Perhaps some coffee?' But, looking around at the heaps of clothes, hats, shoes, and jewellery filling every chair and all the free space in the room, grasped the situation, adding, 'but later. Not now. Yes, of course I'll help. Where do we start?'

Pearl sipped her wine before reaching across the table to the chair facing her, piled high with material. 'This dark red velvet robe is just the job for Councillor Mrs Fowler who's going to open the fair.'

She winked at Lisa. 'Voluminous and sweeping—if that doesn't hide her spreading girth I don't know what will! Just needs the sleeves taking out.'

Lisa smiled, took the dress and examined it. Gratefully her mind switched straight into the coming festivities and she said enthusiastically, 'I'll do the unpicking, if you like. A pity to just carve it up.'

Pearl sighed. 'Thank goodness you're here.

Yes, please do—my eyes aren't up to all that fussy stuff. Now let me see—' She picked up some corduroy trousers. 'Breeches, do you think? Dyed dark blue? Very Elizabethan.'

'Tell me about last year's fair, Pearl.' Lisa adjusted a handy spotlight on to her work and picked up the scissors.

She needed to get Pearl talking to see what she knew about Debbie, this year's Queen. And even if she'd heard anything about the street busker with the guitar . . .

'Well, it rained, didn't it? The heavens opened just as the Queen was being crowned, so all the court fled into the marquee where the eats were waiting and the whole thing was a disaster!' Pearl's laughter was in contrast with her words, and Lisa grinned.

'So let's hope we're due for a heatwave this year. And who's to be the Queen? Anyone I know?' She ripped part of a sleeve out of the dress. 'Always used to have a local girl for the part—still do, I expect.'

Pearl was inspecting some Turkish sandals. 'Flatten the toes and they might look Elizabethan, I suppose.' She glanced across. 'No, not a local this year. Someone called Deborah Standing—I've heard she's a friend of the people up at the manor. A nice child.

'She's been in to see me, asking about lace and other fripperies for her costume. She'll look lovely when she's dressed up. Goodness!'

Suddenly the shoes dropped to the floor

and Pearl stared at Lisa. 'You'll be here this year! Now, what are you going to wear? We must find something very special for you, my love—I think there's a gorgeous old brocade party dress somewhere, very full skirt and low neck—just the job, eh? I'll fish it out tomorrow.'

Lisa started on the second sleeve. 'So what about the men, Pearl? Any takers for handsome princes? Or even—' The words came unexpectedly. '—court musicians?'

'Funny you should say that,' Pearl confided, sipping her wine. 'I chatted to that young busker this morning—the guitarist who plays outside the civic centre. Such wonderful eyes, pale like harebells . . .'

Dreamily she smiled at Lisa who had to stop herself agreeing enthusiastically. Yes, Tom Fallon did have fantastic eyes . . .

Instead, she said, 'Is he coming to the fair, too? The chap with the guitar?'

'He said so. Said nothing would keep him away. Specially when I commented on Debbie being the Queen. Do you know?' Pearl's eyes held Lisa's. 'I think they're close. He knew all about her, and his smile, when he said what a good Queen she'd make, was really something.' Pearl sighed. 'Romantic! You and Martin ought to be like that, you know—I think he needs a good supportive relationship.'

Lisa put the separated sleeves and the remainder of the dress in a neat pile on an

45

already over-crowded chair and stared at them. She couldn't think what to say, and suddenly all her interest in the fair died. 'Can I do anything else for you, Pearl?' she asked stiffly. 'Any more ripping apart—?' That was all she seemed to be good for, these days; ripping apart the old friendship with Martin; ripping up her career. Wishing she might rip away Tom Fallon's relationship with that wretched Debbie . . .

'What's the matter, my love? You sound a bit down.'

Pearl's concern brought a lump to Lisa's throat and she said unsteadily, 'Everything's muddled—I can't seem to get a grip on life at the moment.' Looking up, she met Pearl's gaze and managed a lacklustre grin. 'I think I need some coffee rather badly—I'll put the kettle on, shall I?'

*   *   *

Half an hour later the coffee mugs were empty and the heaps of clothes still filled every space, but Lisa felt better. Pearl's warmth, added to the never-ending gossip flowing out, had brought about a return of more positive thoughts.

Life seemed in proportion again, and she'd learned several interesting titbits of local news that overrode the confusion of her departure from Martin.

For one thing, Pearl told her that the guitar player worked at a market stall with a friend. Always there on a Friday, and sometimes at the Elizabeth craft market on Tuesdays, too.

Lisa straightened her face and stood up. 'Pearl, you've been such a help. I must go now—my turn in the shop tomorrow morning, you see, and I need to talk to Sarah before she goes to bed. I'll run now—thanks again. No, don't see me out . . .'

'Don't forget to come and see about your costume, darling, time flies, you know.' Pearl waved and Lisa left the house filled with new thoughts. She wasn't sure if they were happy ones or not—after all, Pearl had suggested that Tom and Debbie were an item and that was hardly the best news.

And that bit about Martin needing a supportive relationship and what was Lisa doing about it?

'You're late,' Sarah closed the last account book and sat back, sighing. 'Thank goodness that's the last.'

Lisa thought she looked tired and pale. 'Like a drink?' she asked. 'Coffee? Herbal tea?'

Sarah looked at her. 'How nice to be asked,' she said, with a smile that for once actually reached her eyes. 'One of the things I miss when Terry isn't here. He always looked after me, you see.'

Lisa went to the Aga and moved the kettle

47

on to the hot hob. 'Camomile tea, that's what you need. Calming, and it'll help you sleep. Sarah—' Turning, she met Sarah's eyes. 'Can we talk for a bit? Things I need to discuss . . .'

The two mugs of tea scented the kitchen and seemed, to Lisa, to soften the atmosphere between them. She felt Sarah thawing—just a little.

'That traction thing's driving Terry mad.' Sarah smiled over the table. 'He can't even sit up yet, poor darling. Never the most patient man was he? I pity the poor nurses!' She yawned. 'What've you been up to this evening? Is that what you want to talk about?'

'In a way,' Lisa said carefully. 'I had supper with Martin. At his flat. It's nice there—and he's a good cook.'

Sarah's face remained expressionless, and she said nothing.

Lisa tried again. 'I was angry that he organised this business about hiring out jewellery this morning without asking either of us—and specially agreeing that the girl have the Lovers' Knot piece that Dad loved so much.' Sarah just looked down at the liquid in her mug and made no comment. Lisa went on determinedly. 'I mean—he shouldn't make decisions, should he?'

She watched Sarah's face grow thoughtful, even a bit disturbed. At last she said, 'No, of course he shouldn't. But since your Dad died, Martin's been pushing himself here. Learning everything to do with the business. And, of course, with Terry away lately, he's been a terrific help. Quite honestly, I couldn't have managed without him. But—'

The word died into the silence, and Lisa frowned. Martin's plan, when he'd given her the impression that he wanted to take over the business, echoed through her head. She said cautiously, 'He sounds very ambitious these days. I know he's got amazing ideas.' She stopped, and then added, almost to herself, 'Which include me.'

'I see. And what's your reaction to that, Lisa? You're an independent woman, always have been. Surely you won't let him run your life for you?' Sarah, for once, looked really interested.

'No.' It was abruptly crystal clear. 'Certainly not.'

They looked at each other, and then Sarah said, 'But it might be a good idea to go along with him, don't you think? I mean, see exactly what he's up to . . .'

Lisa caught her breath. Spying? Her immediate reaction was to snap, no, but then the sense of Sarah's suggestion dawned, and so she said slowly, 'Yes, I suppose so. But I don't like the idea of—well, being sneaky . . .' She paused. 'You see, I've always been fond of Martin. Still am, in a way.' She frowned. Her muddled feelings were even more confusing now.

'Sneaky? Don't be silly! All I suggest is that you spend time with him and get him to tell you what his plans are.' Sarah looked at Lisa very intently. 'You'd enjoy that, feeling as you do—and you don't need to let it become serious if you don't want to. I mean, you said you were going to pick up the old threads, didn't you?'

'Yes, I did.' Lisa decided and then nodded. 'OK, I'll do my best. But don't be surprised if nothing comes of it. We parted badly this evening.' She frowned. 'Don't ask me why.'

*   *   *

Half past seven, and already the market was humming with people and voices. Cars and vans parked all over the limited space allowed and men and women streamed backwards and forwards, carrying various goods and crafts to the trestle tables already in situ.

It was a moment Lisa had always loved—the feeling of energy and activity, of life in all its different aspects, of ordinary people and just a few not-so ordinary.

The coming together of trades and crafts, the noise of laughter and chat, the constant flow of visitors, all excited her. Even the smells of butchery, fish, and local grown fruit and vegetables added to the general happy hubbub.

There was a slight breeze this morning, but

the sun shone and the faces all around her were bright. She watched Ron Hodges laying out his lovely terracotta pots on the pavement below his stall and had a word with his neighbour, Ruth Sanders, who still sold second-hand clothes, just as she'd done when Lisa was a child.

'Hi, Ruth—remember me?'

The woman's lined, weathered face creased into a smile and she paused in the act of hanging some blouses on a rail. 'Lisa! Heard you were home—and how's that brother of yours? Broken leg, eh?'

A wet nose pushed into her hand and she looked down at the deep brown eyes of Les Stanbury's old dog. 'Sacha! Still going strong, boy? Well done!'

Les turned from his table where he was arranging newly-baked bread of all sorts and shapes, and colours. 'Why, it's Lisa! OK, dear, are you?'

And then, in the middle of telling Les just how OK she was, Lisa saw Tom Fallon. It took a few seconds to remind herself that she hadn't really come looking for him—only a visit to bring back old times. But she walked towards the stall where he stood, talking to a small, stocky man with darting eyes.

'Hi, Tom. Fancy seeing you here,' she said brightly, and then thought, really, what rubbish, when she knew only too well that she'd come specially to find him. What must he think of her?

But he turned aside, smiling as if he was as glad to see her as she was to see him. 'Come to buy some jewellery, Lisa? Good stuff here, I can tell you—Eddie's the king of costume jewellery. What d'you fancy? A tiara?' He picked up a half circlet, letting the sun gleam on the stones encrusting it.

Behind her pleasure at seeing him, Lisa wondered where Debbie was. And why she wasn't using Eddie's excellent make-believe jewellery for the fair.

If Debbie was around, could she ask her? But, glancing about, she didn't see her. And Tom was waiting for an answer. Clumsily, she said, 'I don't think I'm the tiara type. A nice gemstone ring would be more my sort of thing.'

He put down the tiara, took her left hand in his and looked down at her fingers. 'Small, hardworking and worth decorating. Let's see what Eddie's got. What's your birth sign, Lisa?'

Surprised, she said, 'Taurus, but—'

'Right. A beryl or turquoise—take your choice.' Releasing her hand, he bent over the stall, chose two silver rings from a display and held them in front of her startled eyes.

She saw he was smiling, that brief, vivid smile that had captivated her right from the moment they first met. And when he took her left hand again and slid first the pale green

52

beryl and then the turquoise on to her third finger, she felt a great glow of pleasure. Of course, he was only joking, but she had the weirdest feeling that the expression on his watchful face said a lot more than he meant her to know.

CHAPTER FIVE

Tom was looking expectantly at her and Lisa felt stunned—but excited. Did he really like her? Or was he just flirting to pass the time?

'I'll settle for the turquoise,' she told him lightly, removing both rings and giving them back. 'Green's for danger, isn't it? While turquoise means eternity—or something. Doesn't it?'

She was caught by the way he looked at her; his pale eyes were warm and laughing and gone was the shadow that once or twice she thought she'd seen in them. He looked almost happy.

Then the spell broke. 'Well, at least I know how your mind works now,' he said, chuckling and putting back the rings on Eddie's table. 'So what are you doing here? Playing truant from your shop? Not open yet, is it? Or are you leaving that guy, Grainger, to take over this morning?'

Lisa looked at him sharply. Had there been a note of near-contempt when he said Martin's name? But he was smiling at her, adding, 'Let's wander, shall we? Lots of good things to see here.' He glanced over his shoulder. 'OK, Eddie?'

Watching the small man's expression, for a moment Lisa was thrown. She saw unexpected

54

interest flare on his thin, bony face as he stared at her, and then he grinned, waved a hand, shouted, 'Right', and turned back to his wares.

Tom was moving away, so she just nodded, and together they wandered off through the crowds. Throwing aside all the strange ideas and reactions that the last few moments had raised, she remembered she hadn't answered his question, and said, 'Yes, Martin will hold the fort.' She paused for a moment. 'It'll be his turn to come here next—he always spends hours going round the stalls on a Friday.'

'Got lots of friends, has he?' Tom stopped at a table full of tribal art and grimaced at the wooden faces staring back at him. He picked up a dark, evil-looking mask and held it towards her. 'Wouldn't like to meet this guy on a dark night.'

Lisa laughed. 'Nor me,' she said, adding, 'Yes, Martin knows everyone. And particularly the traders who dabble in bric-a-brac and old jewellery. Gets lots of bargains from them— and then sells them on.'

As they wandered on, she glanced round at Tom, saw his dark eyebrow raise cynically, and added, 'That's business for you, I mean, he's an excellent salesman. Oh—' she stopped suddenly for she'd just seen Debbie talking to a woman at the nearby second-hand book stall.

Tom had followed her gaze, raising an arm to wave across the market. 'Hi, Debbie—'

The girl looked round, saw him, nodded and then stared. Lisa felt herself being scrutinised and finally recognised. She felt embarrassed. Debbie, this morning, was back in t-shirt mode, looking as untidy and unnoticeable as she'd been elegant and eye-catching only yesterday.

What was going on, Lisa wondered and then knew she had to find out. 'Back in a minute, Tom,' she said, and then quickly walked over to the stall, caught Debbie's eye, and said, 'Hi! Could I have a word?'

If Debbie was surprised, she didn't show it. 'Right. What about a coffee?' She looked back through the crowds and shouted, 'Are you coming, Tom?'

Lisa was suddenly uncomfortable. But Tom Fallon seemed as unfazed as his girlfriend. 'No thanks,' he called easily. 'I'm helping Eddie out. See you, Lisa—maybe I'll drop into the shop later . . . cheers.' And he disappeared into the throng of people clustering around the stalls.

Lisa felt the joy had gone out of the day and couldn't understand why Tom was so off-hand with Debbie. But Debbie was looking at her and she knew she must get her act together. Find out whether Debbie in her dull clothes was the same girl as Debbie in a neat suit, flirting with Martin and looking sensationally beautiful . . .

'Right,' she said purposefully. 'Let's go—'

56

and led the way through the crowds to the cafe inside the civic centre.

*　　　*　　　*

Debbie drank her cappuccino, sat back and looked at Lisa with a quizzical smile. 'So what's all this about?' she asked lightly.

'Don't you know?' When Debbie just shook her head and drank more coffee, she said firmly, 'Come on! Surely you must realise what a mystery figure you are? I mean yesterday all dressed up and taking Martin for a ride, and then this morning—well . . .' She hesitated. 'Just look at you!'

There was a pause. If Debbie was disturbed, she didn't show it, simply shrugged her shoulders and said, 'You mean my clothes? Well, I'm an actress. I play different parts. Does that answer your question?'

Lisa stared, taken aback. She hadn't expected this easy dismissal of what seemed an off-beat situation. And yet it seemed logical. She narrowed her eyes, mustering her thoughts. 'That's why you know the people at the Manor—they're in show business, too, aren't they—and—yes, I see—why you've been chosen to be the Queen this year . . .'

'Got it in one.' Debbie's voice was casual, but Lisa sensed a note of mockery.

'And Tom?' She hadn't meant to bring him into the conversation but now she had perhaps it was a good thing. Bring everything out into the open and then she'd know exactly where she stood.

But Debbie wasn't playing the same game. 'No, Tom's a musician, not an actor.' Her expression was bland.

'I didn't mean that. I meant—' What did she mean? Lisa drank more coffee and frowned. 'He's your boyfriend, isn't he? I've seen you together . . .'

Debbie smiled, then drawled, 'Nosey little number, aren't you? Well, let me tell you this—sure, Tom's my boyfriend, but just remember that that's my business and nothing to do with you. I mean—' She paused, then added, 'You're Martin's girlfriend, aren't you?'

Across the table their eyes met and Lisa felt a barrier building. She took a deep breath, and said quietly, 'No, I'm not.'

Debbie's smile died. She pushed her empty cup away and got to her feet, her expression sharp. 'OK, you've made your point. Tom's got an eye for every girl he sees . . . well, I haven't got time right now to go into all that. I've got a job to do . . .'

'And so have I.' Lisa rose, they exchanged a last hostile look and then Debbie sauntered away. Lisa walked back to the shop, thinking over this strange conversation.

After a leisurely breakfast, she sauntered into the shop, smiling at Martin who looked at his watch and said drily, 'Good thing I was here to open up . . . business starts at nine precisely, in case you're interested.'

Lisa's resentment rose and she glared. 'Don't give me orders, Martin—I told you last night that this business belongs to Terry and me, not you—'

He held her stare but didn't reply, just turned away, and Lisa was left feeling uncomfortable. She watched him opening the mail and managed to restrain the words that instantly flew into her mind. 'I'll deal with that, if you don't mind . . .'

Then she remembered Sarah's suggestion of keeping in with Martin, or at least watching and listening and trying to pick up what plans and ideas he had about the shop.

After a bit, while Martin, as if reading her mind, handed her the post, she sat down behind the counter and offered him a stiff smile. Somehow she must make amends.

'Sorry about last night, Martin,' she said quietly. 'Must've had a bad day, or something . . . let's try again, shall we?'

He stopped unpacking some old Toby jugs which he said he'd found at Dave's stall and bought for a song—sell them on for a good price, one was a Winston Churchill and the other the Iron Duke, he added—then turned and looked across at her.

His face was expressionless, but Lisa saw his eyes narrowing before answering her, and when he spoke, his voice was warm. 'I'd like

59

that, Lisa. Yeah, got off to a bad start last night, didn't we? My fault I guess. Trying to hurry you along—'

Relieved, Lisa nodded and returned his smile. 'Right. So why don't I invite you to supper tonight? My cooking's not up to yours, but I'll see what I can do . . . Sarah will be at the hospital, so we can have time alone.'

'Great.' Martin left the Toby jugs and came nearer, leaning his arms across the counter and grinning into her eyes. 'Go for a drink first, shall we? I'll meet you at the Cross Keys—OK?'

'Suits me,' said Lisa. 'I'll look forward to it.'

*   *   *

Lisa visited Terry during the afternoon and was delighted to see how much better he seemed. 'Latest X-rays show everything's going on OK,' he told her breezily. 'I've told the doc I plan to be back in the shop at the end of next week—'

Lisa was amused. 'And what does Sarah say? Even if you're out of traction by then, you're sure to be in plaster—you'll blunder into everything—I can see all the china crashing about. Or will you just sit in the kitchen and let Martin and me carry on in the shop?'

'I'll be where I'm needed, love,' Terry said quickly. 'Right there at the front of things. Martin's doing a good job, but I can't expect too much of him for too long. Don't want to overwork him, do I?'

Lisa didn't reply. She wanted to talk to Terry about what she and Sarah suspected—that Martin had plans for a take-over, but didn't know how to start. Terry mustn't be worried; he'd find it difficult enough to be at home again after the safe cocoon of hospital life.

And maybe she and Sarah were wrong—just looking at Martin's behaviour from the wrong angle. But she said at last, 'I think he's enjoying being in charge, actually—just for a week or so . . .' and watched her brother's face.

Terry grinned. 'Bossing you about, is he? Well, that's only natural. I mean, Dad thought he was a treasure from the day he started at the shop after leaving school, and I must say I've found him willing, quick to learn, and responsible. He's having fun, being in charge, I guess. Can't ask for more, surely?'

'No,' said Lisa, and then changed the subject. 'We'll have a party when you come home. Sarah will be ready to loosen up a bit—shut the shop early, and I'll organise something really special.'

'That'll be nice. And make sure you ask Martin . . .' Terry looked at her shrewdly. 'Used to be fond of him, didn't you? Still are, perhaps?'

'Well—' Lisa hesitated. Her brother's eyes were warm, a touch concerned. Quickly she

61

said, 'I've been away—we've both grown up and we're trying to work things out, see how we feel . . . I'm just not really sure . . . nor is he—not yet.'

'I see.' He nodded. 'Sounds sensible. And what does Sarah think?'

'Sarah? About Martin and me?' Lisa hesitated. Of course he wanted to know her reaction—which Lisa felt she couldn't tell him. At any rate, not yet. Not till he was stronger and better able to cope with any doubts about Martin's ambitions. She said lightly, 'Sarah knows we can't do without him, not even with me at home. And we keep him under our thumbs, I can tell you!'

'Poor chap.' Terry laughed.

Lisa leaned over the bed and kissed him. 'Must run now.' Smiling, she left the ward, wishing that she didn't have so many worries nagging at her mind.

CHAPTER SIX

She shopped on the way home, buying salmon and clotted cream and caught the last raspberries in the market. What she'd said to Terry about her and Martin trying to work out their mutual feelings lingered, and suddenly the wanted to get a good meal going this evening. What was that old saying? The quickest way to a man's heart is his stomach . . . maybe today they'd both feel more relaxed. Maybe things were going to work out after all.

Back at home, she prepared the salmon so that it would only need quick cooking later, did some vegetables, eyed the raspberries suspiciously before deciding they looked protein-less, and then hurriedly changed out of her jeans before meeting Martin at the Cross Keys.

'Hi!' He smiled a welcome, and Lisa's suspicions melted. She felt stupidly happy; what on earth had she been thinking of? Martin was OK, not a bit the shady character she'd decided he'd become.

'I'll have a white wine spritzer, please,' she said buoyantly, joining him at the bar.

'You look good—' He nodded approvingly at her slightly outrageous golden printed shirt and even more highly-patterned honey and tan cropped trousers. 'Brought the tropics home with you, haven't you?'

'I guess I have. But Stretton needs bucking up—it's grey and stuck in its ancient past—don't you feel that, Martin?' The wine was relaxing.

'Sometimes. But not for much longer, I hope. Let's sit over there, shall we? It's quieter . . .' He led her to a table by the window, away from the crowded bar and sat close to her on the bench seat.

'Well? Tell me—' She looked at him, smiling, waiting.

Suddenly his mobile rang and he pulled it out of his pocket, turning slightly to one side, keeping his voice down and speaking in short, sharp bursts.

At first Lisa didn't bother to try and listen. But the call went on and then despite her growing guilt, she knew she wanted to hear what it was about. Clearly the caller was no friend—she heard suppressed anger in Martin's voice.

Around the bar a couple of locals were guffawing loudly. Martin spoke very quietly and she only heard a word or two. 'Told you, don't call me here—tomorrow. Jake and Rawlings—right. See you.'

The call ended, he pocketed the mobile and turned back to her, his smile apologetic. 'Someone I gave my number to—shouldn't have bothered. What a time to call! Don't other guys ever have evenings off? Now tell me about Terry. I know you saw him this afternoon—how is he? Coming home soon, Sarah said . . . is that so?'

Lisa had the strangest feeling that she was being guided away from the phone call. In the old days she knew Martin would have been far more honest, exploding into, 'That was Jake, or Rawlings or whoever.' Who are these people, she wondered? Not local names. But here he was definitely changing the subject. Why?

She hesitated briefly and then decided to follow where he was leading. They lived different lives today; if she wanted to get closer, she mustn't start asking awkward questions. Just play it his way . . . 'Yes, he's hoping to get home next week,' she told him. 'If his doctor agrees.'

Wryly, she added, 'I think he's going to be disappointed, but you know what he's like once he makes up his mind. And if his leg is in plaster, that's certainly going to pose quite a problem—he'll have to be careful in the shop.'

Martin nodded, looking thoughtful. 'Better if he stayed away till the plaster's off, then. I mean, we can manage the shop OK without him for a bit longer.'

He put his mug down on the table and smiled at her; just like the old Martin, Lisa thought. Charming, getting his own way. He smiled, as he added, 'I told Sarah there's no need for her to bother, now that you're

65

home—she's got other things to keep her busy. We can cope, can't we?'

'Of course. But—what did she say to that?' Lisa wondered at Martin's audacity, remembering her sister-in-law's suspicions.

Martin chuckled and drank the last of his beer. 'Not much. Just told me that she'd make the decisions, not me! A feisty lady, our Sarah, wouldn't you say?'

'Yes.' Lisa said nothing more. She drank up her spritzer. 'Time to go. I've got to cook when we get back . . . come on.'

*   *   *

The salmon was succulent, the vegetables a worthy garnish, and the raspberries and cream reduced both Lisa and Martin to silence.

At the end of the meal they grinned at each other, poured the remainder of the wine, and retreated to the sofa where they flopped down, giggling over a bit of local gossip that Martin produced.

In the silence that followed, Lisa told herself that this was an important moment. If Martin really liked her, this was his chance to say so—to kiss her again . . . to show his true feelings. She waited, a touch apprehensive, but happily expectant.

Martin's hand reached out and slid around her shoulders. He shifted nearer. 'Something I want to ask you,' he said quietly and she turned, smiling into his eyes. This was the moment . . .

And then—'What're you doing with that down-and-out, Fallon?' he asked.

Lisa stared. She frowned. 'What?'

'You know what I mean.' His arm slid lower, squeezing her waist. 'You were talking to him in the market—'

'How d'you know? You weren't there . . .'

Martin tapped his nose and grinned. 'Eyes and ears. You know how gossip works. And then he came into the shop, asking for you when you were at the hospital this afternoon.'

'Did he? But he knew I wasn't going to be there . . .' Too late she realised she was compounding his suspicions.

Martin withdrew his arm and looked at her frostily, smile suddenly vanished. 'Yeah? So you have been speaking to him. What's it all about then? I think I have a right to know.'

That did it. Lisa moved away, tucking herself into the corner of the sofa, glaring at him.

'Really? And what right is that? Let's get it straight, Martin, you have no rights at all— OK, we were friends before I went away, but that's ages ago. I've changed since then, and so have you—we're independent now, and don't you forget it. And anyway—' She watched a hint of anger slide across his face, but didn't care. 'What's it to you whether I'm friends with Tom Fallon or not? And another thing—he's

67

not a down-and-out, he's a musician . . .'

Martin's expression was sour and she stopped.

'He has no future.' The words were low, the contempt enormous.

She prickled angrily, but knew better than continue this unpleasant tirade. Martin was showing himself in unfamiliar colours, and the fact startled her.

Maybe Sarah had been right, Martin had turned into an entrepreneur whose ambitions exceeded his natural charm and friendliness.

'I'll make some coffee.'

She could stand it no longer, this horrible atmosphere with Martin staring at her as if he were trying to bore into her mind.

She'd hoped for better than this—hurrying into the kitchen she switched on the kettle, then swung round as she heard him follow her.

His voice had lost its usual warmth. 'So you're chasing that down-and-out, are you? Thought you had more sense, Lisa—'

He came closer, hands on her shoulders, turning her to face him as she reached for mugs from the dresser. 'You'll be better off with me.'

She stepped back, dropped a mug, and glared at him. 'Now look what you've made me do!'

But he held her, drawing her close, staring into her eyes with a remembered sensuousness that suddenly silenced her and sent all other thoughts flying.

This was the old Martin whose embraces and kisses had meant so much not so many years ago.

And when he looked at her like this, how could she deny him?

All the anger vanished and her body yielded as his arms pressed her closer. They kissed and she knew she was back in the past enjoying the moment, intent only on sharing everything with him.

For a second, even as she found herself reacting so readily to his kisses, she felt herself at one with the world again; no worries, no fears, just a certain knowledge that life was wonderful, and would continue to be so. All the worries forgotten.

Until he let her go, smiled into her bemused face, and said quietly, 'What did I tell you? Who needs Fallon?'

And instantly she was in the present again, hostility pounding through her head, stiffening her body as she stepped away from him.

For a moment she didn't answer, aware that he stood there, lazily propping up the doorway, watching as she bent to pick up the broken pieces of china at her feet.

She thought rapidly, not knowing what to do or say for the best. And then it came to her. What Martin really wanted was her friendship and support, not necessarily her love.

Support for whatever plan he had in mind

. . . He was just playing games with her. Right, to meet him on his own terms.

As she found another mug and poured the coffee, she slid him a half-smile. 'I can't answer that,' she said jokily. 'We're not that friendly.'

'Yet.' Martin's voice was suspicious, but as she glanced at him, she saw he was amused.

'Tom's got a girlfriend. Debbie—you know, the girl hiring the jewellery . . .' She put the mugs on the kitchen table and pushed the sugar bowl across, gesturing to him to sit down. 'Which reminds me, you never gave me details of that little deal—has Sarah dealt with the insurance cover?'

She sat down thankfully; this was much better; everything back on a business footing.

'Told her I'd do it—save her the trouble. Did it on the phone. It's OK. Nothing for you to worry about.' Martin stirred his coffee and looked thoughtfully into the swirling liquid. 'Debbie said the sun would catch that old piece, make everyone see it. Our little business will be on show, all right.' Suddenly he grinned, eyes gleaming appreciatively.

In her mind's eye Lisa saw the elegant silver pendant, with its huge aquamarine burnished by the sun, and had to agree that it would look stunning on an equally beautiful body. Then she saw Dad's smiling face, looking so admiringly at his favourite jewel.

'I don't know what Dad would say—' And

70

suddenly tears weren't far away. She looked into Martin's eyes and said unevenly, 'I wish I'd been here when he died . . .'

Martin was silent for a moment. His voice was gentle when he said, 'Look, you came as soon as you could. That last illness was very sudden and he didn't suffer much.'

She watched as he looked down at his hands, before adding, 'A great man, your dad. Did a lot for me, giving me a job . . . yeah, great, he was.'

Lisa cleared her throat and sipped the coffee. This was a completely new side of Martin that she hadn't met before. It made her put away the rather awful picture she'd been building lately.

Hastily, she tried to get back to normal after the uncomfortable display of emotion. 'So when is Debbie going to collect the necklace?'

'Not till the morning of the fair. Don't worry, it'll stay where it is, safely locked in that old cabinet, until then.' He smiled at her. 'Forgiven me, have you, for saying she could hire it? I mean, no reason why I shouldn't do so—part of the business, aren't I?'

Lisa hesitated, then grasped the nettle. 'No, you're not,' she said bluntly. 'Like I told you, the business belongs to Terry and me.'

In his turn he paused, before leaning across the table, smiling with all the old charm into her eyes. 'Of course. But look—it's time I told you, isn't it—I want Terry to make me a

71

partner in the business.'

Silence, with Lisa's mind working overtime. Then, aghast, she said, 'But why should he? It's only a small concern—not big enough to expand . . .'

'But it could.' Martin broke in excitedly. His hands drummed the table. 'If it was run by someone with more ambition.' The words tumbled out, the tone firm and sure. 'Terry's a nice guy, sure, but he's lost in yesterday; he'll never make money that way. If I was a partner, I'd be able to introduce new ways, new contacts—new outlets—lots of new money . . .'

Lisa let out her held breath, steadied herself and said, 'What you're trying to tell me, Martin, is that you want the business for yourself. Right?'

Silence while she watched his eyes narrow, saw his mouth firm, finally saying, 'Right, Lisa. And if you and I were really close there'd be no problem in my slowly taking over from Terry, would there? He'd be glad to have me in charge. But I need you, too. We could be terrific together . . .' He paused, then added huskily, '. . . really make something that your dad would've been proud of.'

Mixed emotions churned through her. So here it was, the truth she and Sarah had anticipated and now Martin was saying he wanted her to help him achieve it.

And suddenly she was torn apart by her emotions—Martin wasn't as hard and unfeeling as she'd thought. But she didn't love him. Did she? What was she to say?

CHAPTER SEVEN

The honest words formed themselves slowly but her voice, as she spoke them, as quiet and determined. 'I'm fond of you, Martin—always have been. And I like the idea of building Dad's business, but I couldn't do anything that would upset Terry and Sarah. Surely you can see that?'

For a moment he said nothing, stared into her eyes and leaned back in his chair. Then abruptly he got up, striding to the door, turning just long enough to say over his shoulder. 'No, I can't. I don't want to. I think you're playing games with me, Lisa.' His voice grew angry. 'It's that Fallon guy, isn't it?'

Her heart pounded and she got to her feet, staring at him. 'No, of course not! It's simply that I don't like the way you're treating people.'

He laughed edgily. ' I like that! What about the way you've been treating me? Well, I've had enough. I'll go my own way from now on—you'll see . . .' The door banged and he was gone.

Shakily Lisa turned to look back at the table. Martin had turned back into the old sulky self-willed schoolboy. Her mind whirled and she wished she could go back and say things.

But then she knew she'd been right. His idea of the two of them pushing Terry out of the business was terrible—cruel—and surely quite unworkable.

She wondered wildly what sort of backing Martin had that would enable him to run the shop, even if Terry was agreeable to selling? Did he have financial sponsors? Why hadn't he spoken of them? Then she recalled the phone call. Who were Jake and Rowling? Were they all to do with this wretched plan of his?

She cleared away the dishes and stacked them in the dishwasher, then sat down and watched TV. She went to bed early, and lay awake for a long time while Martin's angry face and even angrier words echoed in her head. It was a long, troublesome night.

Pearl came into the shop next day, her beaming face helping Lisa to smile in return. 'Darling! I've found the very thing for you—the dress—you know—for the fair . . .' She smiled beguilingly into Lisa's eyes. 'Come round when you can and we'll see if it fits . . .' Her smile evaporated. 'Something wrong? You look like—'

'I know, I know.' Lisa cut in quickly, not wanting to know what she resembled at this particular minute.

The mirror had shown her only too well this morning that she was pale, intent and obviously unhappy. 'OK, Pearl, I'll come when I can. Bit busy, right now, Martin's having an hour off . . .'

Thank goodness. The atmosphere between them had been uncomfortable since the shop opened and she'd been thankful when people drifted in fairly regularly and she was able to avoid his frozen face and resentful eyes.

'Right.' Pearl nodded, long earrings swinging wildly. 'And another thing—that lovely man, that guitar player, you know, with the harebell eyes . . .' Clutching the counter for support, she beamed even more broadly. 'Can you believe it, he wants a costume too! Well, I said, of course, let's see what we can find . . .'

She looked all set to go on for another half hour so Lisa smiled wanly, and murmured, 'Sorry Pearl, I've got customers to deal with. See you later . . .'

'All right, love.' Pearl went out like a whirlwind and the shop seemed larger and emptier after she'd left. But Lisa found she could smile again and even consider what the day might hold . . . yes, she'd go and see Pearl later on.

She went directly after lunch and he was there—Tom Fallon of the harebell eyes, guitar slung over his shoulder, chatting away to Pearl as if they were old friends. As Lisa entered the dark, crowded little shop, he turned, and his smile sent her worries flying.

'Hi, Lisa. Great to see you—got the afternoon off, have you?'

Slightly dazed, she looked first at Pearl, who

76

nodded encouragingly, and then back at Tom. 'Well, no, just a couple of hours . . .'

He walked briskly to the door, held it open and then looked back at her. 'Long enough. Come on, I've borrowed some wheels, we'll be there in just over ten minutes . . .'

'Where?' All thoughts of the dress Pearl had found evaporated, and Lisa, feeling in a daze, followed him outside, where he linked her arm in his and strode quickly down the street, grinning at her amazed expression.

'Something I want you to see. Something you'll enjoy—and remember. You know what?' He was very close, his eyes inspecting her intently. 'You look as if you could do with a treat—everything OK, is it?'

'I—' No words suggested themselves, so she simply nodded.

'Good. Business running well? Martin making profits for the firm? And how's your brother?'

She was so surprised by the flow of questions no answers came. Instead she found she was smiling, really smiling, no more stiffness, no more worries—just smiling at Tom and thinking what fun this was. On their way to somewhere . . . together.

At the bottom of the town they turned into the street where he lived. Tom stopped beside a snappy little red MG, parked his guitar on the back seat, and said, 'Hop in, Lisa.'

'I didn't know you had a car—' Carefully

she avoided any question of busking and being on the poverty line, but Tom's answering grin showed that he clearly understood what was in her mind.

'Like I told you, a friend's letting me use it while he's away. Now then, hold on to your hat . . .' He drove out of town like a streak.

'Where are we going?' She felt a part of whatever adventure Tom was embarking on. Abruptly she realised she hadn't been so happy since coming back to Stretton.

'Wait and see.' His sideways smile increased her enjoyment and so she simply watched the scenery racing by as the car headed out into the countryside.

*   *   *

When he braked outside an entrance with huge stone pillars topped by twin eagles, she caught her breath. This was familiar— somewhere where she and Terry had explored when they were small and allowed out on their bicycles. A huge country estate, long neglected, but now apparently rehabilitated.

Tom drove down the long drive, finally stopping in a car park half-hidden behind huge shrubs. 'We're here. Out you get.'

Smiling, not saying any more, he led her out of the car park and down the immaculate lawn stretching ahead. Lisa, hugging herself as the happy memories grew more and more vivid, laughed. 'I know! This is Farham House. I've been here before, when I was a kid. It was a ruin then—Terry and I used to get in through that wood over there . . .' She pointed, and suddenly Tom caught her hand.

'House-breaking? I wouldn't have believed it of you. Well, it's all legal today, the gardens are open to the public and I wanted to see them—with you.' He glanced down at her, his smile gentle and just a bit amused.

She took the bait. 'Why with me? What've I got to do with gardens, for heaven's sake?'

'Because you must be an expert—seen them all, haven't you? All over the world? France, Italy, California . . . ? Well, let me tell you, this one beats the lot. And this is the time to come—mid-June, rose time in England, you see . . .'

'Rose time?'

He took her hand and swung it, smiling at her ignorance. 'I've brought you here to change your mind about the grass being greener on the other side of the world—and certainly greener than here, in dreary old England . . .' She was ready to argue, but he just grinned and went on. 'I know, I know— you're a seasoned traveller, you've seen it all— but just wait.'

They turned a corner and then Lisa stopped, eyes wide, amazement and intense enjoyment filling her. Roses filled the space ahead of them. Great sprawling bushes, covered with blooms that shone in the sun and wafted clouds of fragrance all around.

Wine-coloured roses, purple ones, bright pink, pale pink, yellow, white . . . huge open blooms alongside delicate, clustered flowers. Lisa realised Tom was right. She'd never seen anything quite like this before.

Suddenly she realised Tom was watching her. He pointed to a rose beside her. 'Souvenir de la Malmaison, blush pink and beautiful,' he said. 'Just to remind us of the Empress Josephine and all the roses she grew while she waited for Napoleon to come home from war.'

Lisa sniffed the rose and was impressed. She laughed. 'OK, you win. This is just wonderful. I could go on looking at them for ever. Oh, this fragrance!'

Slowly she wandered along the lush borders, amazed at the wealth of colours and the enveloping sweetness. By the time she'd reached the end of the rose garden, she felt light-headed.

So much blossom, such scents—the very air was drenched in fragrance and she was grateful to Tom for bringing her here.

She turned. He sat on a bench beneath a wall festooned with languorous, pale petals, watching her. She saw him rise, saunter towards her, and, with a sudden intake of breath, realised just how deeply she was attracted to him.

Even the knowledge of Debbie and their

relationship couldn't diminish her happiness at that moment. She went to his side, smiling into his expectant eyes.

'It's fantastic, Tom—brilliant! I've never seen anything like it—you're right, nothing can beat this. Even here, in dull old Stretton . . . Thanks for bringing me.'

'My pleasure.' He took her hand again, nodded towards the grey stone house that provided an elegant backdrop to the riot of colours in the garden, and said, 'Fancy a cup of tea? They do a nice line in home-made cakes in the café . . .'

'What a good idea. I feel quite spaced out with all that amazing colour and smell . . .'

*   *   *

The tea-room was old-fashioned and cool after the heat of the afternoon sun. Lisa chose a small table beside the window and Tom ordered a cream tea. 'When in Rome,' he said lightly, and Lisa laughed, finishing off, 'When in Devon eat all that clotted cream . . .'

They'd finished their scones, cream and homemade raspberry jam, and were lazily sitting over second cups of tea, chatting over various foreign holidays they'd both enjoyed, when Tom asked casually, 'So what's your friend, Martin, doing this afternoon?'

Lisa was surprised. 'Martin? I've no idea. Minding the shop, I hope.' Then she saw an odd expression on Tom's face, quickly veiled, but enough to make her add, more sharply, 'Why do you ask? What's Martin got to do with you?'

Tom shook his head, again seemingly merely amused. 'Not much. Just a conversational gambit, I guess.'

He looked across the table and his voice lowered. 'What I really want to talk about is you, Lisa. About us. I mean—here we are . . . But maybe I'm out of turn . . . You and Martin are close, aren't you?'

It seemed that the sun's warmth and light had suddenly diminished. Lisa leaned back in her seat. Carefully, she said, 'We're old friends. Went to school together. Then my dad took him into the shop . . . yes, I suppose we were close in those days. But now—' She stopped.

Tom was watching her very intently and she guessed that her eyes had told him more than her words. Suddenly it was important to let him know the truth—but did she know it herself?

After a moment, she added slowly, 'Martin says he's fond of me,' and then halted. She heard her voice grow suddenly defensive. 'Look, I don't think it's any of your business, actually.'

Tom seemed unaware of her discomfort. Casually, he said, 'I suppose not. But here we are, you and me together, and I just need to know the score.' He grinned. 'I don't want Martin accusing me of taking his girl, do I?' He laughed, and Lisa saw how warm his eyes were and felt herself responding to the half-said invitation.

She could have asked him, in return, about Debbie, but her thoughts were full of other ideas, other images, other needs.

Tom's undoubted charisma hid his shabby clothes, and the long, curling hair that so badly needed cutting. His warmth and his low, deep voice with its crisp accent had become strangely necessary to her.

But he was only a street musician, a down-and-out with no real job. She saw his hands clasped on the table in front of her, large, strong, beautiful hands, and felt her body react . . .

Confused, she forced her mind back to Martin. Talk about Martin. That'll take Tom's attention away from me. He seems interested in Martin. Now, what to tell him?

It wasn't difficult. 'Like I said, Martin and I went to school together,' she said gratefully, sitting back and keeping out of Tom's reach.

'Dad took him into the shop as a trainee and he stayed. He's good in the shop, you see . . .' She watched Tom relax in his chair. 'He's very knowledgeable about antiques in general. Terry relies on him a lot, you know.'

'And you—do you know much about them?'

Thank goodness he was following her lead.

'Not a lot,' she said. 'I was never very interested—not even in school holidays when I sometimes helped Dad out.'

He was looking at her quizzically. 'Which is why you went off and travelled?' His smile flowered. 'Sensible girl.'

'I love my job.' Enthusiasm kindled new warmth in her voice. 'And I'm longing to get back to it.'

'When your brother's better. So you'll be off on your travels again then?'

'Yes—yes!' Memories spun; sunshine on glistening water in the Med; hot dry winds blowing up a sandstorm around the desert; even the misty rain of a soft day in Ireland would be more exciting and fulfilling than dear old boring Devon.

And then the perfume from a raspberry-pink rose swaying just outside the window suddenly swamped all the longing that was filling her.

For here she was with Tom and she felt ridiculously content. Perhaps, after all, she would stay here once Terry had recovered—if Tom was still around . . .

His deep voice brought her back to reality. 'But before you can dash off again, you've got an amazing day ahead of you. Surely the Elizabethan fair in the grounds of a very old ruined castle must be something to be reckoned with?'

She knew he was teasing her, smiling, she

said, 'Of course. I'm to be a lady-in-waiting and Martin says he's a foreign prince come to win the Lady!'

'That's Debbie.' Tom nodded, grinned. 'She's very excited about it—a part she's never played before, she says—and, of course, the costume's gone to her head. All she can talk about is that amazing dress—apparently Pearl's really gone to town with it—and then that fabulous necklace . . .'

'Yes,' Lisa agreed. 'She'll look really good. Let's hope the sun shines.'

Tom was silent for a moment. Then he said slowly, 'It's a magnificent piece from what she told me. I can't wait to see it for real.'

'It's silver,' Lisa said, easily visualising it. 'A big lovers' knot beneath a square setting with a huge pale blue-green aquamarine in the middle. It's gorgeous.'

Lovers' knot—and suddenly she recognised that that's what she was caught up in—a knot, holding her between the possible loves of Tom and Martin. She snatched a breath and then looked away, before Tom could ask what was the matter.

Forcing her memory backwards, she saw her dad holding the treasure, his face full of respect and admiration. For a second she wondered if he'd hate the idea of it being shown to the public in this way.

Then she remembered Sarah's annoyance, and added, 'Sarah, my sister-in-law—was terribly upset when Martin agreed to hire it out. Said it was too valuable, but of course he talked her round. Said it would be terrific PR for the shop.' She realised she was talking herself around, too, so added hurriedly, 'Got the gift of the gab, has Martin. A real salesman.'

'Yeah. He did a very astute deal with me over my gold Hunter,' Tom agreed. He leaned back in his chair, stretched long legs and added casually, 'Guy like him—clever, young, got a good head on his shoulders—you know, I'd have thought he'd be up in London or somewhere, making the big time, not stuck down here. What keeps him in Stretton, Lisa?'

'Me,' she said spontaneously, and then frowned. 'I shouldn't have said that. No, what Martin really wants is to make something big and successful out of our little business.'

She thought for a moment and something new surfaced. Slowly she added, 'He wants to do it because Dad was so good to him . . .'

'With you to help him.' It wasn't a question, more a bold statement of fact.

She sighed, recognised that the truth was out and wished she'd held her tongue. But Tom was easy to talk to and it had seemed only natural to tell him all about it. It was almost as if he'd put a spell on her.

Sharply, she said, 'That's enough about me. If we're playing truth games, Tom, it's your turn now—' Her eyes challenged his. 'So tell me about you.'

'Not much to tell.' Smiling at her, he looked relaxed and easy, a man at peace with himself. But instinct told her differently.

She leaned over the table, looking into his eyes. 'Of course there is. All sorts of things I want to know about you—'

'Ask away.'

Did she imagine it, or had his smile lessened? She said quickly, 'Where do you come from? How did you learn to play the guitar so well? And what about the roses—you seem to know all about them—I mean, they're not ordinary ones, or are they?'

'Hey, one at a time, please! I come from the London area—tell by my accent, surely—and I teamed the guitar at school. As for the roses, well, I once worked in a garden where my boss told me all about the old shrubs and species . . .'

He grinned at her. 'Particularly about Napoleon's girlfriend, the Empress Josephine, and her passion for roses. That answer your questions?'

She sighed. Clearly he didn't intend to tell her anymore. Nothing about how he lived now, nothing about Debbie. She got to her feet. 'I think I ought to get back, Tom—my two hours must be up. Shall we go?'

Beside her, he paid the bill and then, abruptly, the noise of a siren filled the café.

Instinctively, they both turned and listened,

87

then walked down the garden towards the car park. The siren had stopped and Lisa said, 'Thanks for bringing me. I really enjoyed . . .'

As they turned into the car park, the words died. Beside the red MG two police officers stood, eyeing the car and making notes. One of them looked up as Lisa and Tom approached. 'Good afternoon, sir. Is this your vehicle?'

Lisa watched Tom's face change from smiling ease into tight wariness. 'Yes,' he said shortly, and stood silently facing both policemen.

Lisa was bewildered. What did he mean, it was his car? He'd told her it belonged to a mate and that he had permission to drive it. So why this obvious lie? She reached out her hand and touched his arm. 'Tom—?'

He frowned at the question in her voice and shrugged away her hand. 'It's OK, Lisa, nothing to worry about. Now, see here, Officer . . .' Turning, he walked away a couple of paces, and she realised he didn't want her to know what was going on.

Anger burst through her confusion and she felt herself tense. Was Tom, like Martin, a man playing games with her emotions? Well, if so, then this must be the end of it.

Quickly, mind made up, she turned away, marching back up the garden, heading for the public phone to order a taxi to come and take her back to Stretton. Tom's voice came after her—'Lisa, hang on—' but she took no notice.

The taxi ordered, she strolled back through the rose garden, trying hard to concentrate on the flowers and forget Tom's deceit. She even picked a particularly beautiful pale pink rose, hoping the gardener wasn't looking.

It was a sort of comfort, its fragrance and old-fashioned beauty helping to swamp the emotions that struggled through her waning self-control.

Pausing at the bend in the rose garden, she saw the police car drive away, heard Tom call again and then saw him striding towards her. 'Lisa—everything's OK. I can take you home now—' He stopped in front of her, smiling as if nothing in the world had happened.

But, to Lisa, everything had happened, she avoided his eyes, said tightly, 'No thanks. I've got a taxi coming—it'll be here in a minute. No need for you to bother,' and then stepped past him, walking down the drive towards the entrance, and praying that he wouldn't bother her further.

He stayed where he was, and she felt his eyes—his blue, blue eyes, shadowed now, she was sure—following her as she walked away. But he didn't try and stop her, didn't even try and explain. Clearly, he realised it was all over between them.

As she got into the taxi, the rose in her hand was trapped between her and the door handle. She moved it free and felt a thorn prick in her finger. A tiny drop of blood fell on her trousers when she sat down, and she looked at it in horror.

So there was a dangerous side to old roses, was there—in spite of all their beauty? Like Tom—a handsome, desirable guy, but with a hidden past he wouldn't talk about.

She was thankful to pay off the taxi and get back to the safe, small world of the shop, where Martin was already looking at his watch and remarking that it was past four and where on earth had she been?

'Learning things about life,' she told him soberly, refusing to respond to his knowing grin as he said smartly, 'A bit late, isn't it? Got to be savvy these days, you know—the world's busier and more dangerous than it was when we were at school.'

'Yes,' Lisa said, watching him as he left the shop. 'You can say that again.'

*   *   *

She visited Pearl after she and Sarah had shared their evening meal, and Sarah had left to see Terry. Pearl was, as usual, immersed in clothes, sewing machine whirring away on the kitchen table, and a bottle of wine at hand.

'Darling! Come for your fitting? It's right there—see—the green one on the hanger on the door . . . slip into it and see what it looks like. Lovely material, and that colour really

90

shows up your hair . . . wine, darling?'

'Why not? Thanks.' Lisa took a glass with her into the small room opening off the kitchen, which acted as a fitting room. She hoped the wine would give her back the ease of mind that the afternoon had stripped away. Of course it was ridiculous to feel as she did, upset and hurt by Tom's deceit. But there, he was a man, and everyone knew that men didn't see things like women did. Or feel as deeply . . .

She stepped into the dress, drawing it up over her shoulders. Lisa looked into the mirror and suddenly felt worlds away from antiques and dangerous, thorny roses.

The dress was clothing her with a new found elegance and dignity that jeans and T-shirts never did. She was smiling as she stepped back into the kitchen and met Pearl's critical eyes.

'How do I look?'

'Gorgeous.'

Startled, she stared at the figure just coming through the doorway. 'Martin!' Suddenly it was a relief to see him there, good old Martin, someone she had always been able to rely on.

CHAPTER EIGHT

She smiled across the room, chuckling as she saw the unfamiliar clothes he wore. 'So you're in your Elizabethan gear, like me?'

He grinned, made her a dramatic bow, and fingered the starched ruff around his neck. 'Can't wait to get out of it, actually. But you really do look something—'

His green eyes were warm and appreciative, and Lisa enjoyed the obvious admiration.

Swishing her full skirt around she watched his eyebrow raise, and said lightly, 'Don't worry, no chance of seeing an ankle beneath this lot. But if you wait for Pearl to make sure it's all fitting OK, I'll get back into today's gear.'

Pearl interrupted. 'Everything fit all right, Martin?' and he nodded.

'Yeah. Only this scratchy old ruff's a bit of a nuisance.' He looked across at Lisa's green silk dress with its jewelled sleeves and bodice, and then said quietly, 'How about we both get changed and then go on?' Ignoring Pearl's wide eyes he added, 'A movie? A bite to eat? A walk—'

'Lovely,' Lisa decided at once. 'It's such a super evening—let's go along the river path to that pub in Rushton.' She looked back at Pearl. 'I'm thrilled with all this glamour but please can I take it all off now? Think I'd rather live today than yesterday!'

'Turn round and just let me see how the back falls . . .' Quickly Pearl was on her feet, inspecting the beautiful dress . . . She touched the material, folding it into a richer ripple of decoration, and then nodded. 'Fits well and looks wonderful. Yes, darling, take it off.'

As Martin disappeared into the adjacent sitting-room, Lisa skipped back into the tiny fitting cubicle and changed back into her own trousers and T-shirt.

She felt relaxed, slightly excited about the coming fair, and definitely happy that she and Martin were friends again. For the moment she even forgot about Tom Fallon.

Back in the kitchen, just as Lisa was tidying her hair, Pearl said, 'Evening off? That's nice. Going well with you and Martin, is it?' She beamed and the sewing machine was silent for a moment. 'Just what you both need, like I said, a proper, supportive relationship.'

'No lectures, please,' Lisa said lightly, her hand on Pearl's shoulder. 'But thanks for the costume, it really is brilliant. I'll be here early on Saturday morning. Anything I can do in return?'

Pearl's lined face grew soft. 'Just enjoy yourself, my darling. And don't listen to any rumours.'

Lisa paused by the door. 'What rumours?'

'If you haven't heard any, then I'm not

saying.' Pearl's smile widened. 'As you know, I'm no gossip . . . Off you go—'bye.' And once again the sewing machine started to purr.

Leaving the shop together, Lisa and Martin headed for the river. There was little traffic in the streets, but suddenly an open red sports car raced past them, its driver raising a hand in greeting.

Lisa tensed, and Martin scowled. 'That's Fallon, isn't it? Where on earth did he get that car? Bet he's up to no good . . . I've heard a thing or two about him around the town.'

Lisa looked at him. 'What things? What d'you mean?'

Martin shook his head, and she got the impression that he clearly wished he'd said nothing. He took her hand, smiled determinedly and said, 'Only the things they all say about buskers: nothing you want to hear about. So let's talk about something else like what we'll eat at the pub!'

They laughed and walked on in silence for a moment or two and Lisa finally pushed away the realisation that Tom must be playing some sort of game and Martin didn't want to bother her about it. So forget Tom.

Here she was with Martin and the evening was magical, he was in a good mood, the sunset colours were gentle, and the whisper of the cool breeze relaxing.

Their walk through the woodland, and the river chattering and gleaming in the soft evening light was wonderful.

Lisa put aside the niggling worries, even forgetting momentarily that wretched confrontation with Tom earlier today.

She linked her arm with Martin's and felt a new rapport building between them.

Martin was chatty. 'Remember those old Toby jugs I picked up yesterday?'

She nodded. 'Sold, are they?'

'I did a great deal. And the guy bought several other bits, too. I took nearly five hundred pounds.'

Her eyes widened. 'Five hundred? Martin, that's brilliant! That'll help Terry's deficit, won't it?'

For a second she sensed him hesitate. Then he said briskly, 'You bet. Well, p'raps not quite five hundred, just under . . . so yeah, he'll be really pleased.'

He grinned at her enthusiastically. 'So we're back to being friends, are we? And have you thought any more of my plan about the business? You know, Lisa, I don't mean to cause any trouble to poor old Terry . . . how is he, by the way?'

'Sarah said the traction's ending tomorrow and after that he'll be in plaster. He's decided he'll come to the fair in a wheelchair—' She chuckled. 'Guess who'll be wheeling it?'

'Me, I suppose,' said Martin resignedly.

She pressed his arm. 'I'll take turns. And he's not too heavy . . .' Thoughts of the fair whirled around her mind. 'Have you seen Debbie again?' she asked. 'I suppose she's got her costume all ready—and you'll take the necklace to her in the morning? Has she signed the agreement Sarah prepared?'

Martin increased his stride. 'Hey, come on, don't let's talk shop. Yes, yes, everything's under control.' Then his voice lightened and he grinned at her. 'Hurry up, I'm starving.'

*　　　*　　　*

The Fisherman's Arms was noisy and crowded, so they took their bar snacks outside, where tables stood beneath shadowy trees and privacy surrounded them.

Martin drank his beer and watched as Lisa sipped at her white wine. She saw his eyes growing very intent in the dusky light. 'There's something I have to tell you—' His voice was quiet, lower than usual.

She put down her fork and looked across the table. 'What is it? You sound—well, worried . . .'

She watched him attempt a grin, fail and then lower his head. For a frightening moment he looked quite unlike the Martin she thought she knew.

She tried a joke. 'Don't tell me you've lost the famous necklace!'

To her amazement, he simply stared at her without replying.

Her voice fell. 'Martin, what is it? For heaven's sake, tell me . . .'

'I've been a bit—silly.' He picked up his knife and started toying with the meal on his plate.

After a moment his eyes met hers. 'This is hard to say Lisa, but—well, I'm in a spot of trouble—heavy trouble.'

Lisa laid down her fork and tried to steady her breathing. She looked at him very closely and saw anxiety in his eyes.

'Tell me,' Lisa said again, and waited. Thoughts of Sarah's suspicions and Pearl's rumours raced through her mind, as well as Tom Fallon's repetitive questions about Martin.

Where did all this fit in? What had Martin been up to? And how bad was the trouble—? Suddenly, her emotions swung around and she felt angry. For heaven's sake, why couldn't he run his life properly without all these hitches?

'Ever heard of selling-rings, have you?' he asked after a long pause, and there was a new, hard note to his voice.

'In the antiques business, you mean?' She kept very calm. 'Yes, Dad told me about them. A few dealers ousting others at sales. Keeping prices high when they're not worth that much. Cheating on other dealers. So what about them?'

He sat back, ignoring the plate in front of him.

97

'That's it. A lot of racketeers on the make. Well, that's what I'm involved in. Only I made a mistake once and I want to get out now—but they're blackmailing me to do a last trick for them. Or else there'll be nastiness.'

Lisa felt her blood begin to surge. She faced the fact that all along she'd wondered about Martin's methods of buying and selling, but hadn't had the courage to face the truth.

If she'd know earlier, maybe she could have helped him. She took a deep breath, and said slowly, 'So what can you do to get out of it? Surely there must be a way—' and watched his face slide into anger.

'I know I was daft to get in with them in the first place, but, honest, I don't know how to get out now.'

'Can't you go to the police?'

His laugh was harsh. 'You must be joking! No, I've got to play it more cleverly than that. See, Lisa, I did wonder if that Tom Fallon was involved, and if so—'

He leaned across the table and then stopped as someone called from the entrance into the garden—'Hi, Martin!'—and he sat back, frowning into the twilight.

'Debbie—'

She came across, a plate of sandwiches and a glass in her hands, smiling at them both as if they were old friends. 'Just the guy I wanted to see—mind if I join you?'

Lisa nodded stiffly and Martin said at once,

'Course not. What's up, then?'

Debbie sat down, put her plate on the table and looked sideways at Lisa. 'Didn't expect to see you here,' she said provocatively. 'Thought you and Tom might be off somewhere. He's got this car he's borrowed—can't keep out of it.'

Lisa said nothing. If Debbie thought she would rise to such crude bait, she was wrong. Tom and his car—and was it really borrowed, or not?—were in a different world from Martin and all his problems. Or were they?

She sat back and listened while Debbie began telling Martin why she needed to see him.

'It's like this. I've heard a rumour round town that your fabulous aquamarine necklace isn't real. That someone's made a paste copy of it, and that's what I'll be wearing tomorrow. Which—' Debbie swallowed a mouthful and stared accusingly at Martin, '—isn't right. I gave you that cheque for the hire of the real thing, not a dress-up copy and I need to know that you and your shop aren't playing games with me.'

She took a drink of her fruit juice and bit into another sandwich, still staring at Martin.

Lisa acted quickly. Before he could reply, she leaned forward and said carefully, 'But your cheque didn't go to Martin, you know, it's been paid into our bank—the bank who deal with my brother's and my business.'

She slightly emphasised the words and had the satisfaction of seeing Debbie look puzzled.

'OK,' said Debbie, narrowing her eyes. 'So you've got it, not Martin. Well, it doesn't matter to me who's the boss around here, all I'm concerned with is that someone's playing a nasty trick on me and my charitable sponsors who paid for this PR exercise in good faith—and I don't intend to let it go on.'

Lisa looked at Martin.

He'd gone pale and was fidgeting in his chair.

'Martin,' she said gently, 'Tell Debbie that she's wrong, will you? Just clear all this up, please.'

'Paste copy?' he said jerkily. 'Don't know what you mean. Absolute rubbish. You'll get the necklace—the real thing—on Saturday morning, just as I told you. And anyway—'

Suddenly his voice rose and Lisa saw his expression grow more hopeful. 'Who started this rumour? Got a name, have you?'

Between mouthfuls, Debbie started laughing. 'A great friend of yours, actually, I'm afraid. One Pearl Adams, the costume-lady who seems to know exactly what's going on in the town. Surprised, are you? I'm not. I've met her sort before.'

Lisa got up. Pushing back her chair she met Martin's surprised eyes, and said quickly, 'I'll take myself off home. I need to talk to Sarah. You stay here.'

The words hung in the air. She saw Debbie's eyes suddenly narrow and focus on Martin's face. He half-rose, nodded at Lisa, started to speak, and then stopped. He sat down again and stared at his uneaten meal.

'See you in the morning, Martin. Cheers—' Lisa didn't waste words on Debbie, but knew an amused expression watched her walk away.

CHAPTER NINE

Lisa went quickly through the darkening woods, keeping to the safety of the path and telling herself that somehow she must find a way of helping Martin out of his self-induced problem.

A paste copy of the necklace? Her thoughts flew back to the market stall and Tom helping Eddie who made cheap but realistic copies of jewellery. Was that really what Martin had done? Cheated on everybody concerned by copying the necklace, and planning to give it to his blackmailing pals to sell?

But she didn't think it was all that valuable—from what she knew of the antique business, villains like the ones Martin was involved with were into the big time, making millions, not just hundreds. No, it couldn't be that . . .

And then another, terrible thought swept into her mind. Tom, helping Eddie out—did that mean that Tom, too, was involved in all this cheating? Martin had said that there were rumours about Tom . . . Just for a moment she stopped, appalled by the awful images and ideas that surged but then, somehow, she made herself think of other things. To imagine Tom a cheat and a crook was too painful.

By the time she reached the town fringe and

was back among busy streets, her head had cleared a bit and she went up the high street, heading for home, making herself sort out all the facts so that she could tell Sarah without too much muddle. But just as she reached the lane leading to the back door of the shop, she heard footsteps behind her and glanced around.

'Tom!'

At her side, and without the customary smile, he said curtly, 'We need to talk, Lisa. Anyone at home?'

'Yes, Sarah is.' Lisa stepped away, grasping the threads of her fading self-control. 'But she and I've got things to discuss right now—important things. Can't it wait?'

'No.' He reached out and took her hand and his touch made her body ache. 'I won't keep you long, but no, I can't wait. How about a stroll up to the castle? No-one about up there.'

She nodded doubtfully. Tom was the last person she needed to be with. Even if he wasn't involved with Martin, he'd certainly proved himself to be a liar and seeing him again, feeling his hand on hers, just for this moment, had made her feel confused and weak.

They walked in silence down Castle Street and found a secluded bench among the ruins. Then Tom half-turned and looked at her. 'Lisa, this is hard for me—but I have to warn you that Martin's playing a particularly nasty game, involving your business.'

'Oh!' It wasn't what she'd expected. She took a deep gasp of breath and tried to restrain all the fermenting words that ran around her mind. She swallowed and looked up into the starlit sky, avoiding Tom's watchful eyes. 'I know about Martin,' she said numbly. 'I don't need you to tell me.'

Then she stared round at him, anxiety getting the better of her. 'And how do you know? Rumours, I suppose? Debbie said that Pearl was the gossip-monger. Did she tell you, too?'

He frowned but didn't answer the question. She saw his jaw tense. 'Is Debbie with Martin?'

Anger slowly replaced the mixed-up, longing thoughts coursing through her. But anger was better than unhappiness. 'Yes,' she said shortly. 'Making a play for him, I'd say— well, sounds as if it's all over between you two, doesn't it?'

Tom looked intently at her. Then, gently, he said, 'There's a lot you don't understand, Lisa. So much I can't tell you, I'm afraid—'

She interrupted, anything to stop the threatening breakdown of her control. 'Don't bother! I just wish to goodness we'd never met—that you'd never come into the shop, that Debbie hadn't hired the necklace . . .' Suddenly she choked. 'And, oh, how I wish I'd never come home . . .'

Then his arm was around her and she

104

wanted, more than anything in the world, to rest against his shoulder. As he drew her close, she tried to draw back, but gave in as his hold on her tightened. 'Lisa,' he whispered. 'Don't wish that. Because, if you hadn't come home, we'd never have met. And I'm glad we did. Believe me . . .'

She felt his hands cupping her face and just for a second she thought everything was going to be all right. Martin was only being his old schoolboy self, getting into scrapes, and as usual, she was helping him to escape from them. Tom wasn't really just a busker, but someone playing a joke and he was about to tell her how he loved her, and then she'd say that she loved him, too . . . and then.

But then reality returned and she knew that was all just a childish dream. So she edged away from Tom and struggled to her feet. 'Look, I've got to go. I want to talk to Sarah . . . Goodnight, Tom—no, don't bother, I'll see myself home . . .'

Yanking her hand free, she was out of the Castle Green and heading for the main street before he got up, calling after her as she ran. 'Lisa! Lisa—wait—'

But she didn't. She couldn't. All that mattered was getting back to the shop and locking the door behind her, at the same time banishing all the dreams and longings that Tom Fallon created in her every time they met, and especially when they were apart.

Fiercely she told herself she must concentrate on now, and what was happening, not what might be—but never could be. So tell Sarah about the necklace. Everything else could be forgotten.

Sarah was in her bedroom but she answered when she heard Lisa's call up the stairs. 'I'm here—yes, of course, come up. Bring a cup of something, I've got mine.'

With a mug of camomile tea in her hand, Lisa sat on the big bed in Sarah and Terry's room, and looked at her sister-in-law, sitting in front of the dressing-table.

Sarah's dark hair was round her shoulders, and in her pale, flower-printed satin dressing-gown, Lisa thought she looked far more attractive than usual. Something about her expression—not so taut, much happier . . . well, thank goodness for that.

Wishing she wasn't the bringer of bad news, Lisa asked gently, 'Terry on his way home, is he?'

Sarah applied cream to her face and massaged it in with slow strokes. She smiled into Lisa's reflection in the mirror. 'Yes,' she said simply, and Lisa heard a warmth that had been absent from her voice ever since she came home.

'Good. And he'll be able to come to the fair?' Finding it hard to get to the nitty-gritty of Martin's stupidity, she knew she was filling in with commonplaces.

106

Sarah nodded. 'He's quite determined. And good old Pearl's being marvellous, says she can find him something to hide his plaster in but still look the part.' She grinned at Lisa.

There was a comfortable pause between them, until Sarah wiped her face, swivelled round on the stool and looked at Lisa keenly. 'What's up? You don't normally want to chat at bedtime—something wrong?'

Lisa swallowed the lump that suddenly filled her throat. She'd never imagined that Sarah might turn out to be an ally. 'Yes,' she said wildly, and then heard it all tumbling out. 'Martin's done something incredibly silly, Sarah, he's got involved with some villains and I can't help thinking it's all to do with the aquamarine necklace we're hiring out . . .'

It was a relief to tell someone, to let loose all the ugly facts and the ridiculous ideas and worries that were filling her mind. She talked non-stop for a couple of minutes while Sarah sat and listened.

Then, reaching for her cup of chocolate standing on the dressing table, Sarah said slowly, 'You poor thing. I didn't know you felt so worked up about it all. Why didn't you tell me earlier?'

And then flushed, looking down into the cup. 'Well—we haven't exactly been close friends, have we?'

Lisa said stoutly, 'Never mind that now. The thing is that we've got to do something to help

Martin to get out of this selling-ring's clutches. And if he really has swapped the necklace for a paste replica, then he's gone beyond the law and he'll be in terrible trouble if it's discovered.'

Sarah nodded. 'Silly boy. You know he's been siphoning off small amounts of money for ages—ever since your dad died? I told you there were some discrepancies in the book, well the accountant found them all yesterday.'

Lisa's heart sank, but then she said numbly, 'I suppose he's been trying to save up to buy the business . . .'

They looked at each other askance, and then began to laugh and Lisa felt her tension ease. 'Sixpence a week for fifty years sort of thing?' she chuckled. 'And that's why his flat is divided between his mum's awful old bits of furniture and one or two very nice pieces. He must have invested his ill-gotten gains in antiques, easy to sell when necessary. Honestly, what a prat he's been! Well, he's learned his lesson now, all right.' Soberly, she looked into Sarah's abruptly unsmiling face. 'But what can we do?'

'Right now, nothing.' Sarah got up, walked to the bed and sat down beside Lisa. 'It's late, we both need our sleep because tomorrow's bound to be a difficult day with Terry coming home.' She paused. 'But the local Police Inspector is the dad of one of my pupils—I could put in a word in Martin's favour, perhaps.'

Lisa nodded and then was cheered enough to joke, 'Terry coming home? Help!' Weakly, they grinned at each other and Lisa got to her feet. In the doorway she looked at Sarah, turning back to the duvet and getting into bed. 'Sleep well,' she said.

'Thanks. Lisa—'

'Yes?' She wasn't prepared for the next question.

'What about that Tom Fallon?'

Lisa caught her breath. 'What about him?'

Sarah hesitated. 'I rather thought you found him attractive. Pearl told me . . .'

Lisa exploded. It had been a long day and this was too much. 'I don't care what anyone in this dump says,' she flared. 'No, I don't think anything of Tom Fallon, and Pearl can just shut up and mind her own business.'

She watched Sarah conceal a smile, as she hastily nodded and said, 'OK. OK, I get the message. Now go to bed and calm down. Night, Lisa . . .'

CHAPTER TEN

Hazy sunshine swamped the busy streets on the morning of the fair, and Lisa felt the heat growing as she changed into her Elizabethan gown, carefully adding the elegant French hood, edged with pearls and backed with a short veil, that Pearl had made to go with the dress.

But all she could think of was the business of the paste copy of the necklace. Had Martin already handed it to Debbie? Would Debbie realise it wasn't the real thing? And if so, what would she do? The idea of losing the lovely necklace haunted Lisa's mind.

She hurried away from the Costume Emporium—important to return to the shop and see if Martin had come to a decision. After all, he'd had twelve hours in which to think about it.

Sarah was on her way to collect Terry from hospital, with a large parcel in the car. 'Terry's disguise,' Pearl had said, grinning exuberantly. Sarah was already in her costume, a demure schoolteacher in her plain print dress and neat cap.

She found Martin in the shop, his face serious. He scratched his neck where the ruff irritated. 'This dressing-up is all a load of rubbish—'

'Don't be a misery,' Lisa told him sharply. 'It's all in a good cause—you know the fair is for charity. Now, tell me what you've done about the necklace.'

'It's here, in my pocket.' To her horror he pulled it out, unwrapped, for all the world to see. The solid silver setting glinted in the sun, emphasising the shape of the lovers' knot, and once again she thought how well it emphasised her own unhappy situation.

'Martin! For heaven's sake—anyone could take it.' She couldn't believe he was still being so careless. Her voice was hard, full of horror, and he stared at her, eyes narrowed.

'OK, OK, so I've made a mistake—but it's still safe, isn't it?'

'For how much longer? When are you supposed to hand it over to that awful man?'

Martin stamped across to the window, thrusting the necklace back into his pocket, staring down the street as he did so. 'When the Queen gets crowned,' he said roughly. 'Everyone'll be looking at her wearing the paste copy. Rawlings'll be behind the pavilion, he'll get away easily.'

The name rang a bell. 'Rawlings . . .' Of course—the phone call at the pub. Lisa knew now that she would never love Martin, but he was her friend, and she would do all she could to help him—as she always had.

'Cheer up,' she said firmly. 'You know what you've got to do, surely—give Debbie the real necklace and forget Rawlings. If he's the crook you say he is, he won't dare accuse you of anything.'

Martin nodded, slowly. 'Wish I was as optimistic as you, Lisa . . . but what about all the other things? Once Terry finds out what I've been up to in the past he'll give me the boot.'

'Which you deserve.' Lisa looked in the gilt mirror at the side of the shop and straightened her hood. Refusing to let herself brood on the future, she managed a mocking grin and then headed for the door. 'We'll each have an hour off, shall we? That'll take us up to eleven, when the crowning's due, and we'll shut the shop for the rest of the morning. I'll go now— OK with you?'

Martin nodded resignedly. 'Thanks, Lisa. You're a good friend. But I still don't know what to do.' He smiled, a travesty of his usual grin. 'And take care—Rawlings is a menace.'

'Don't worry—I've got a dagger in my petticoat,' she told him, more lightly than she felt, and went out of the shop, joining the noisy crowds thronging the street leading to the castle ruins.

*　　　*　　　*

The old stones could hardly be seen now. Huge tented pavilions covered the grass around the dais where the throne stood.

Colourful banners whispered in the summer breeze, and already the smell of roasting meat from the spitted sheep at the back of the green filled the air.

In one corner musicians were tuning up, old-fashioned viols and dulcimers sounding unfamiliar and evocative.

Lisa passed the crowd of men pulling on ropes to hoist the maypole and smiled at old George Farding, swaying in time with the music squeezing out from his accordion.

Then she saw a wheelchair in the distance and ran towards it. 'Terry?' She laughed aloud as she realised how clever Pearl had been. From his falsely tonsured head, down to the soft leather shoe on the leg that stuck out from beneath the clerical grey robe, Terry was disguised as a stiff-legged monk. 'Bless you, my child,' he intoned solemnly, grinning at the same time.

Behind the chair, Sarah joined in the mirth. 'Wonderful, isn't it? Trust Pearl to come up with the goods.' Straightening her face, she said to Lisa, 'Can I let you do the driving for a bit? The kids are waiting for me to organise the maypole dance. I'll be back afterwards.'

'Don't hurry.' Lisa watched her walk away and then pushed the wheelchair to a shady corner. Terry seemed in fine form. 'This is terrific. Said I'd be here, didn't I? And you look brilliant, Lisa.' His smile faded. 'Martin in the shop, is he?'

113

She nodded, fiercely hoping that he wouldn't ask any awkward questions—hurriedly, she said, 'How about a cup of something? If I go and find some coffee, do you promise not to go away?'

'Chance'd be a fine thing,' he said lightly.

Tensely, she headed for the refreshment tent. But music, laughter and voices checking the tannoy system made it impossible to think of anything except the moment. So when, out of the blue, a hand descended on her arm, she swung round, unfazed.

Tom Fallon's cool blue eyes looked at her, widened and then softened. 'You look—terrific,' was all he said, but it was enough to set her heart racing.

'Not so bad yourself,' was all she could find to say in return, because words had almost deserted her. He looked quite different, and even more handsome than she remembered, in the totally unexpected dark suit, matching pale shirt and tie, and with newly cut hair. She tried to cover her astonishment. 'Actually, I thought you'd be a court musician . . .'

'Not today.' He reached for her hand and let her through the throng to a quiet space behind the fortune teller's tent. Then he stopped and looked at her very intently. 'Lisa, where's Martin?'

Her stomach knotted and she pulled away. 'In the shop, of course.'

'He's not.' The low voice was sharp. 'I've

just been there. There's a notice saying it's shut for the rest of the day.'

'But—but we agreed—' She was dumbfounded.

Tom stared at her, and she thought she'd never seen him look so grim. 'It's important that I find him, Lisa. Try and think where he might be.'

Her mind spinning, worried sick about the fate of the necklace, she said, 'No idea. Probably here somewhere. I don't know why he's shut the shop. He shouldn't have done.' She shook her head helplessly. 'I don't know, Tom.'

'Right. I'll just have to keep looking.' He turned away but she snatched at his sleeve.

'Tom—what's this all about? Why is it so important to find Martin?'

For a second he hesitated, but then he shook his head, said 'Sorry, Lisa,' and walked away through the crowds.

Her mind filled with apprehension. Why had Tom suddenly become someone else? A terrible thought surfaced, could he actually be Rawlings? Did he expect to meet Martin behind the pavilion as the Queen was crowned, and take possession of the aquamarine necklace?

Back at Terry's wheelchair with two mugs of coffee, she made a lame excuse for having been so long and was relieved when Terry merely smiled, saying he'd been too busy watching everything to notice. As he drank his coffee, he gestured towards the dais, where preparations for the crowning were going on.

'Has Martin handed the necklace over to the girl?' he asked.

Lisa took a deep breath. 'I'm not sure. If you're OK here I'll just go and find him—see that it's all organised properly . . .' She hurried away before he could ask anything else.

Suddenly the children's dance music began and she saw Sarah lead her little troupe of boys and girls, all dressed in Elizabethan dress, out of the tent and on to the green.

Ribbons hanging from the top of the maypole wove in and out as the children danced. The music lifted and the watching audience smiled and clapped.

And then she saw Martin, walking rapidly towards the crowning pavilion. Forcing a way through the crowds she reached him as he was about to disappear around the side of the tent. 'Martin—stop!' Her voice was shrill and urgent.

He paused impatiently, frowning at her. 'What's up? I'm in a hurry.'

'You shouldn't be here. I left you in the shop.'

'Yeah—sorry, but this is more important than an extra hour's trading—and anyway, no one's about in the town. They're all here.'

The maypole music finished to loud applause, and then a trumpet sounded a fanfare, turning all heads towards the pavilion.

Martin looked at Lisa. 'The crowning ceremony,' he said huskily. 'Well, Debbie's got the necklace...'

'Which one?' Lisa's voice was thin and her heart raced. Had Rawlings got away with it?

But Martin didn't answer, for a dramatic voice came over the tannoy. 'Ladies and gentlemen, this is the moment you're all looking forward to—the crowning of this year's Queen—Miss Deborah Standing.'

'The real one, or the copy?' whispered Lisa and then gasped as Debbie appeared, spectacularly beautiful, with the sun glittering on the famous silver Lovers' Knot and the huge green aquamarine.

This couldn't possibly be the copy, Lisa thought, her mind whirling. She turned to Martin, but he'd disappeared. Staring around, she saw no sign of him. And then Tom Fallon pushed through the crowds, pausing at her side. He said urgently, 'I think we need to find a place to talk, Lisa. I've got to explain everything to you ...'

He found a cool, quiet spot, away from the dais and the watching crowds, and turned her towards him, looking intently into her eyes. 'First of all,' he said gently, 'I'm not a busker. Not a down-and-out. Nor am I a criminal. Does that make you feel better?'

She nodded, too confused to answer and he went on, 'Actually, I'm an undercover insurance investigator. I work in London for a firm dealing in historical collections of jewellery.

'You see, we were told of a possible sighting of a famous necklace in Stretton, and also a warning that someone was about to steal it. So I came down, with Debbie as my assistant. And no, we're not an item . . .' He grinned. 'Busking seemed appropriate to Stretton so I brought my guitar with me. And then, looking for Martin, whose name had been slipped to us, I met you . . .'

Lisa was stunned. She felt as if the ground under her feet were moving. She shook her head in amazement, and Tom continued, his voice low. 'I knew at once things were going to be more difficult than I'd supposed. Lisa, I wanted to tell you everything right from the start, but of course I couldn't.' He stopped, drew her towards him. 'Start again, can we, sweetheart? Pretend this never happened? Now that you know I'm not a criminal.'

When she didn't at once reply he added, almost whispering, 'I love you, Lisa.' She saw the truth in his eyes and it was easy then to say what had been locked away in her heart until this moment.

'And I love you, Tom.'

They kissed and the world stopped until they parted, and then Lisa thought again of Martin—and the necklace. She clung to Tom. 'What happened? Is Martin all right—did he?'

Tom smiled. 'Stop panicking. Everything's sorted out. Martin had the sense to let Debbie wear Eddie's fantastic paste copy of the necklace and took the real thing to the police, who informed me at once. And two officers were sent to keep that rendezvous with one Cyril Rawlings behind the pavilion!' His eyes twinkled. 'But there's a bit more—you see, the necklace itself is very important historically.'

'Tell me.' She wondered what else could possibly happen on this unbelievably happy day.

'The piece was originally commissioned by King Edward the Seventh—for one of his mistresses.'

'Of course—the Lovers' Knot!'

'Yes, and although no-one else knew, inside the hollow silver knot is a message in gemstones,' Tom paused. 'It says "dearest".' He finished quietly. 'Quite a love story, isn't it? And now the piece is going back where it belongs—in the Royal Collection. You and your brother will get compensation, of course.'

They looked at each other. 'My dad would be so pleased to know all this,' Lisa murmured. 'And he'd have been pleased with Martin, too—after all his silly escapades, I mean, actually having the guts to go to the police . . .'

Smiling, their arms entwined about each other, they sauntered back to the noisy throng milling around the fairground. She glanced at Tom mischievously. 'I think I need a long,

119

relaxing holiday after all this,' she said. 'How about us both going somewhere hot and sunny and leaving dreary old England behind?'

'I thought you'd never ask ...'

And then Tom stopped by the ice-cream stall grinning at her. 'Fancy a Neapolitan Bon Bouche to celebrate, sweetheart?'

*   *   *

The celebratory party that Lisa had promised Terry took place out of door. The town was still full of noise and the fireworks threatened to go on all evening, but here, in the cool woodland beside the river, was the ideal picnic place.

Pearl was there, and so were Debbie and Martin. Terry sat in his wheelchair talking to Tom while Lisa and Sarah handed around the eats and filled the glasses.

Listening to the voices rising and falling, Lisa sighed happily as she sat down beside Tom. Never, in her wildest dreams had she imagined that things would end like this.

Then, as if reading her mind, Terry raised his glass and looked at her. 'So I'll be losing my business partner again, shall I, love? Sarah and I have just thought it all out. I've told Martin I'll forgive and forget.'

Martin smiled through the shadows of the overhanging branches. 'Never thought I'd get off so lightly,' he said, shaking his head

120

soberly, 'but doing the right thing worked out OK in the end. Rawlings was caught, and I'm in the clear. And good old Terry understands . . .'

Lisa nodded. 'I'm glad,' she said simply, and watched how Martin turned to Debbie, the expressions on their faces telling her suddenly that they were becoming close.

Turning, she saw Tom watching her. 'Let's walk,' she whispered.

Leaving the picnic party with only Pearl noticing and smiling as she caught Lisa's eye, they wandered down the river path until the voices and the laughter could no longer be heard.

Beside them the water splashed and bubbled, and Lisa, in Tom's arms, murmured, 'We've got to be together, my darling, but your job's in London and mine takes me all over the world—how are we going to manage it?'

'We'll think of something,' he responded warmly. 'But for the moment why don't we let the future look after itself?' And gave Lisa no chance to answer.

*   *   *

The airport was as crowded as usual and Lisa kept glancing at her watch. All her party present except for number twenty-five, and the plane would take off in a few minutes.

Despite her momentary worry, the old thrill

had returned—wonderful to be back in her job, excited and keen to take her party to the Greek island of Skiathos.

Warm, lazy days among emerald hills and sun-gleaming sea . . . and then the lingering evenings with bouzouki music and fireflies lighting the shadowy darkness.

A last glance across the crowded airport, and there, as last, was number twenty-five—tall, floppy-haired again, a handsome man in shabby chinos and a pale sports shirt, backpack over one shoulder, guitar slung over the other, whose blue, blue eyes met hers as if in a world of their own.

Pushing through the crowds, Lisa reached his side. No need for words, just hand reaching for hand, and a feeling of shared happiness. Smiling, she led him towards her waiting group of fellow holiday-makers, knowing that their future rolled ahead of them, unblemished and certain.

The story had come to its fairytale ending. She and Tom were together now, their own particular Lovers' Knot safely and joyously tied.